A Murder of Crows

A MURDER

OF CROWS

An Anthology of Short Stories and Novel Exerpts from young writers in Offaly and Westmeath

Westmeath County Council
Offaly County Council

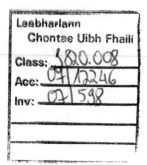
A Muder of Crows

Published by Westmeath County Council and Offaly County
Council in 2007.
ISBN-13: 978-0-9513775-5-0

Edited by Caroline Barry
Subediting and proofreading Neil Richardson

Illustrations by Andrew Murray

Book design and layout by Lir Mac Cárthaigh

A Murder of Crows

CONTENTS

Caroline Barry

EDITORIAL

A*Murder of Crows* is a collection of novel excerpts and short stories by young writers in counties Westmeath and Offaly. It is the second publication to be produced as the result of a joint arts initiative between Westmeath and Offaly county councils.

A Murder of Crows is the largest anthology I have edited to date, and sadly I could not include all the writing submitted to me during the year. The participants were extremely industrious, supplying me with several pieces each. I chose work that would highlight the young writers' talent and give the reader a flavour of the unique styles being developed by these young midlands authors.

It has been a great pleasure to work with such talented and dedicated students. Some may go on to have careers as writers, others may not. The whole point to writing is to discover the magical landscape within, to grapple with the psyche and to explore the discarded or hidden material of the unconscious. Our responsibility as writers is to find our creative voice and tell a good story. The young writers in this book have begun this exploration of the imagination, and hopefully it will give them confidence in their own ability, no matter what they choose to do in life. I wish them luck and have every faith that they will succeed.

I would also like to thank Catherine Kelly, the arts officer of Westmeath County Council, and Sinead O'Reilly, the arts officer with Offaly County Council for their kind support and encouragement. Without their vision this project would never have been realised. I would like to also thank Andrew Murray for his wonderful artwork, Neil Richardson for second proofing the manuscript and Lir Mac Cárthaigh for designing the book.

Niamh Morgan

SURGICAL STEEL

Kilbeggan Writing Group
16 years old
Chapter one of her novel
Surgical Steel

Connor sat slouched on the rigid, hard backed chair, examining his shoes. He had never considered the purpose of shoes until now. His shoes weren't like everyone else's, he grinned to himself, revelling in the fact that even in footwear he managed to rebel from the norm. Lost in this thought, the click of the office door behind the chair startled him. Connor's mother emerged along with Connor's principal. Scowling at both of them, Connor listened as the principal boomed in his pompous voice.

"As you well know, Mrs. Fields, we have done everything in our power to facilitate Connor's artistic skills. And for him to repay us with such..."

The principal paused.

"...such disturbing graffiti. Well, it's just not acceptable."

Connor laughed to himself. He felt like saying, 'that pentagram was better than any sappy pictures the art teacher ever got us to draw.' But he bit his tongue.

"I... I know. I'm so sorry, Mister Hayes. I don't know where he gets it from. He had a very religious upbringing; in fact, we always brought him to church. He used to love it, when he was younger that is. Imagine trying to get him into a church now, ha, ha."

His mother let out a nervous laugh. Connor rolled his eyes. Here she goes again, he thought. The principal looked at Connor's mother with distaste.

"Yes, well, Mrs. Fields, but the fact of the matter is that Connor needs a good talking to, not just about his behaviour, but his whole outlook on life. Can I trust you to do this?"

Connor's mother looked as though she would cry.

"Yes, yes, I will," she replied weakly.

Connor stood up and began walking towards the school exit. His empty steps echoing in comparison to his mother's hurried clicks. Sitting beside her in the car, Connor counted to five in his head. Exactly on cue, his mother's shrill voice came across the car.

"Connor?"

"Yes?" Connor replied coldly.

He could hear his mother taking a breath.

"Connor, this is serious, you know what pressures I'm under, what with the new baby and your father..."

She was cut short by Connor.

"He's not my father."

His mother looked worriedly at.

"Well, with Jim being away. I just can't handle everything, and instead of helping you decide to go and get in trouble. It's too much, Connor. You need to cop on and grow up!"

She finished, put on her seatbelt and started the car. Connor looked out the window trying to hide his anger. He couldn't wait to get home, just so he could go out again. Intense joy, what felt like a million spiders crawling across his skin, hit him as he thought of the weekend ahead. He would be free for two whole days.

Connor pulled open the front door and ran up the stairs. He reached his bedroom door, burst in and slammed it behind him. Flinging his schoolbag on the ground, he sat himself down in front of the mirror and began making himself look like the real Connor Fields.

First, a layer of black eyeliner was applied. Then he began with the piercing. A nose ring, an eyebrow bar and few studs in his ear and he was starting to feel more and more like himself. He jumped out of his school uniform, grabbed his trademark black jeans and black t-shirt combo. He glanced in the mirror.

Not very creative, he thought, but it'll have to do.

Connor spiked his messy black Mohawk into place. Like the rest of Connor's appearance, he could only wear it like he wanted to at the weekends. Adding the finishing touch – heavy black new rocks – he grabbed a hoodie and a rucksack and thumped down the stairs, slamming the front door behind him. He wasn't bothered about telling his mother where he was going. He was afraid of what he would say and she'd know well enough where he was off to. Nothing mattered now anyway, nothing except getting on that bus and getting into town. Slinging his bag onto his shoulder he began to walk.

His appearance drew the usual looks as he walked through the village towards the bus stop, which was just across from the local Garda station. When he was safe from prying eyes, inside the bus shelter, he lit up a cigarette. Taking a drag he exhaled a sigh of relief. Checking his watch he realised he was ten minutes early. Each of these ten minutes would feel like forever to Connor. He looked around at what was his hometown, two grocery shops, three pubs, a post office and of course the Garda station. The recent building of two estates had brought plenty of new blood into the village. None to Connor's taste though.

Two girls Connor recognised from school walked around the corner towards the bus stop. Connor surveyed them with disgust. They were dressed in the painfully stereotypical white tracksuit and white runners. They didn't look too impressed by Connor either.

"Goth," came Connor's way in a thick Dublin accent.

"Go fuck yourself," Connor stabbed back.

"Ouuh! Watch it, Sarah. He'll suck your blood," one of the girls giggled to her friend as they walked off

Connor shook his head. He had to stop letting people get to him. The evening sun glinted into Connor's eyes. He withdrew further into the bus shelter, stubbing out his cigarette he checked his watch. Two minutes. Connor's phone buzzed in his pocket. He pulled it out and checked the screen. It was his mam. The bus pulled up. Connor pushed the 'end call' button and jumped on the bus. As soon as he had paid his fare and sat down, a rare smile spread across Connor's face.

The weekend was here.

He was escaping.

Danny leant with his back against the cafe window. Glancing across the road he saw the lights starting to come on in the town park.

Jesus, he thought impatiently, where are ya, Connor? He stood up and walked over to the bus stop. A middle aged woman stood looking him up and down before sniffing. Danny noticed this and smiled. He was no stranger to dirty looks. In fact, he thrived on them. Humming away to himself he pulled out his phone and checked the time.

Oh, Lord, he thought, why does it take so long for a bus to drive from... He paused mid-thought. Where does Connor live again? Now that he thought about it he didn't know. Connor always came to him.

Connor tapped his foot impatiently on the bus floor.

Fuckin' temporary lights, he cursed. The bus had been stopped for five minutes now and Connor was getting restless. His phone went off in his pocket for the second time that evening.

It better not be her again, he thought, while taking it out of his pocket.

A message from Danny. Connor smiled. Danny Moran, his partner in crime and his one and only true friend.

God, thought Connor, how sad am I?

But it was true; Danny was the only person Connor had ever connected with in his life. Thinking of connections, something in Connor's mind clicked.

Shit! he thought, I forgot my charger.

Glancing out the window he realised they were at the army barracks. He started a new text on his phone.

B der in 5. Gotta go, dud. Battery nearly ded.

Connor selected Danny's name from about five in his phone and pressed the send button.

Beeeep.

The sound of his phone dying.

Great, he thought, that puts me out of reach for the weekend.

Realising the meaning of these words Connor smiled and looked back out the window.

Danny's phone vibrated just as Connor was getting off the bus, walking towards him. Connor looked the same as ever, tall and sombre, surveying the people around him as though they were mad.

"Well, hello there, Mister Fields. How are you on this fine evening?"

Connor looked at Danny sceptically.

"I hate myself and I want to die, but we are having great weather. You?" came Connor's sarcastic reply.

Danny laughed and they started walking. Connor couldn't help feeling those spiders again as he looked around the town and realised that now he was really home. Danny's excited voice interrupted these thoughts.

"Aah, Dude, guess what I did today?"

Connor hit the button at the pedestrian crossing and sighed.

"Brain transplant?" he guessed.

"No, smartass. I finally did it. I just went ahead and took the plunge!"

Danny turned around and grinned manically at Connor.

"Move," hissed Connor, jabbing Danny in the back as the lights beeped and went green.

Once they were both safe and alive on the other side of the road, Connor looked at Danny bemusedly.

"Here, Danny, don't mean to be rude or anything, but what the fuck are you on about? Plunged into what?"

Danny stopped walking and began to slowly roll up his sleeve.

"Look," he said, revealing an angry red patch of skin on his wrist covered in cling film.

The word *Sorcha* was etched onto it.

"Ah, I see," Connor exclaimed. "Your mam's on your wrist. But hey, will that not be a bit of a turn off for the girls?

Danny considered this.

"Nah, they'll think it's cool that I respect my mam so much. Trust me, it's a win-win situation."

They passed Dunnes and were turning left down the alley, every step making Connor feel more and more at ease. Danny reached the red door and buzzed the intercom. Connor looked up and read the familiar 'Ink-Corporated Tattoos' sign above the door.

"Who's there?" came a voice from the little steel box.

"It's me and Fields," Danny replied.

"Oh, right, come on up," the voice echoed dreamily back.

The door buzzed. Danny pushed it open and they started up the stairs. As they passed the tattoo parlour the comforting noise of needles and the harsh smell of disinfectant woke Connor's senses and made him feel like there was a set of drums in his chest. Walking further up they reached Danny and his mam's apartment.

Entering the apartment was like walking into Aladdin's cave. Pushing through beaded curtains and hazes of incense, they came into a relatively normal kitchen. Connor seated himself at the table and started flicking though a magazine.

"Tea?" Danny asked, as he rooted through the presses behind him.

"Yeah, go on," Connor answered. "Have you got Jaffa cakes?" he asked while trying to interpret some weird anagram in the magazine.

Danny loved puzzles.

The kitchen door opened and Danny's mam Sorcha walked in, depositing a leaflet on Connor's lap.

"Have a look at that, petal," she said in her quirky English accent. "Make me a cuppa, Danny. I'm exhausted."

And with that she walked out of the kitchen.

Connor examined the leaflet.

Gathering at the church. 8pm sharp. Live bands.

"Here," Danny handed Connor his tea. "Anything interesting?" he asked, nodding at the leaflet.

"Church party," Connor replied.

"Really?"

Danny seemed interested.

"Tonight? Let's go."

"Ah, Danny, you know what goes on there, it's not worth the effort," Connor protested.

"Connor, man, we're the only freaks in this town who haven't been to the church. We have to go," Danny pleaded.

Connor drank a mouthful of tea and looked at Danny.

"I'm not going."

"We're going, pretty boy."

Aisling Daly

GRAFFITI

Kilbeggan Writing Group
15 years old
Chapter one of her novel
Graffiti

A glaring January sun entered unmercifully through the cracks in the window pane and caressed Martin's face. At the top of the street a police siren rang a warning to the early morning arsonists and gangsters that it was time to disappear. The siren startled Martin from his fitful, dreamless sleep. He was unimpressed to find that yet again he had somehow managed to wake up on the stone floor, and when he lifted his calloused hand to the back of his head, a painful lump was warm at his fingertips. He stared blankly around the room in a daze as he was not yet fully awake. The Bacardis from the previous night were taking their toll.

There was nothing in the room worth gazing at. The walls, painted in a dull, cream colour, were blemished with damp and neither a clock nor a picture adorned them. A rickety table and three chairs graced the corner. Martin's bed, unmade and forsaken, lay beneath the window, beside an ancient cabinet that caused a blizzard of dust every time an elbow or leg brushed against it.

Deciding that sitting on the floor and staring at the wall was not a means of helping him escape from reality, Martin struggled to stand up and staggered clumsily into the cramped bathroom. He turned the tap on over his shaking, cupped hands and splashed cold water onto his face. He examined his appearance in the mirror, which was an unusual practice for him. The extra-strong hair gel that he applied yesterday was still intact in his oily, raven hair so it was unnecessary to apply more. The lads told him that the extra strong stuff would last longer, easing the trouble of obtaining money to pay for it. An angry case of acne had proceeded to attack his face and a tiny scar, which was a result of a primary school brawl, was just visible over his right eyebrow.

"Jaysus, Martin," he exclaimed to himself. "Ya look like shite," he continued, staring into the mirror. He had begun to daydream when the sound of Tina and Paul Larrigy's six young kids running around in No. 263 next door suddenly woke him from his reverie.

"Feck it!" he exclaimed.

The noise of the kids running around next door was an indication that he was late. Martin scampered out of the flat, forgetting to shut the door behind him, and hurried down the stone steps at the end of the corridor, almost knocking over Mr. Ward who was leaning against the iron railings and having his morning fag.

"You watch where you're goin' in future or I'll stick my fag up you."

Martin blocked Mr. Ward's husky voice out of his ears, his mind was too occupied with other concerns to worry about the rants and raves of an old man who he could easily beat up. He stumbled onto the dirty street on reaching the ground floor of Sacred Heart Heights. Even though the sunlight was strong, there was an icy bite in the air. The sirens had stopped by now and everything was back to normal.

Standing in the middle of the street and looking all around him, all Martin could see was a large group of children racing after a makeshift ball and a heavily pregnant woman sipping on a can of cider. He shook his head.

She wasn't here.

Martin let out a sigh, knowing he now had to search the entire surrounding area for her. He jogged briskly through the blocks of flats avoiding all passers-by as he had no time to chat or argue. The minutes ticked by and the morning was hurrying on. He searched almost every nearby alley, street and apartment block, bellowing her name as he went. By now his heart was beating so hard that he could nearly see the veins tremoring in his thin wrists. She never ventured out this far, and he was convinced that the worst had happened. Sitting down on an old bench and lighting the Benson he had saved in his pocket to calm his nerves, he faced up to the fact that he would have to search St. Mary's Gardens as he was aware that she was physically unable to travel any further. St. Mary's Gardens had a reputation of being the roughest area of flats in all of South Hill, and possibly the whole of Limerick City. Martin had heard many stories of gory gangland murders occurring here. Standing up and stretching, he mustered up the courage to make his way through the area, making his best effort not to delay or hesitate.

The flats were almost near collapse and every window was either smashed or lacking glass. Colour was non-existent here, creating an eerie aura which Martin felt prickling his skin and entering his clothes uninvitingly. The place was peculiarly yet hostilely silent, and a group of skinheads huddling in a doorway threw him a piercing stare, letting him know that he was not from these parts so he was not welcome. Martin endeavoured to avoid their gazes and marched on up the street, throwing his shoulders back with each step. It would be a huge mistake to show these men that they unnerved him. He refused to be an easy target for them and admonished himself. As a fifteen year old was now well capable of going everywhere without fear.

It was then that Martin caught sight of the woman of the hour, lying miserably beneath a rotting bench. Crying out her name, he crouched down beside her and placed a hand on one of her shivering shoulders. A half-empty bottle of Powers whiskey was tight in her grasp and four fags lay smouldering by her brittle, auburn tresses which were quickly greying at the roots. He realised that she had run out of cocaine, so he was aware that she would be difficult this morning.

"Wat brings ya out 'ere, Ma?"

"Watsit to you?"

Ignoring her demanding enquiry, Martin gently lifted his mother up, turning a deaf ear to her swearing. Throwing her arm over his shoulder, he headed for home.

"Get the fuck off o' me! What ya come all the way out 'ere for anyways?" she challenged him after five minutes of cursing to herself.

Martin sighed heavily.

"Well I don't want ya gettin yourself raped or killed or anythin' now do I?"

She thought for a moment as they drew nearer to the Sacred Heart Mansions.

"Well I don't need any help off ya, so why don't ya do somethin' better and go to school or somethin' like dat?"

On returning to the 'Mansions', Martin savoured the street he lived on. Compared to the Gardens, it was bliss. The flats were built from red brick, but many of the bricks had loosened or fallen off Each block was separated with either a patch of green or a street, and abandoned flats were boarded up forlornly. A group of lads Martin's age whom he recently had a fight with hurled stones at him as he struggled towards the door leading up to the flat, while supporting his mother's thin frame.

"How'z your ma, Marto? Ya bollix!"

Martin suppressed the seething anger he felt at their jeers. He would deal with it later. It seemed like weeks had passed before he climbed those long, stone steps and travelled along the noisy corridor to No. 262. He carefully guided his mother into her cold bedroom and helped her onto the bed. It was somewhat of a miracle that the place was not trespassed as Martin had left the door ajar, not there was a lot to rob or vandalise. Not another word was shared between mother and son and as Martin gave him one final look, he left as if the events of the morning had never occurred.

He contemplated why his Ma was so important to him, because for as long as he could remember, the morning routine had been the same. When he found her each morning, her dull skin would be sallower than the previous night, and her temperament edgier as a result of her nightly binges and doses of whatever illicit chemicals took her fancy, but it was usually cocaine. At times he was convinced that she was unaware who he was as she always seemed so distant, so insipid. Oblivious to who his father was, Martin pondered over who he really was, and where he came from.

"Pah!" he grumbled, kicking an empty coke can and observing it skim the road with a klink. "Watsit all bout?"

Suddenly, he found himself entering the room in his head occupied with dark, taunting thoughts – the taunts that reminded him that he was worthless and there was no point in making a go of life as nobody cared.

Then he got inspiration.

A sudden rush of adrenalin caused Martin to whip out the can of spray paint that he kept with him at all times and run to a patch of wall free from graffiti. He started to spray every thought in the dark room onto the wall.

"Untouchable. The forgotten are the ones who su!er in the dark. My inner voice speaks to the wall."

He continued spraying words over words until his work became illegible.

When the can was empty he stopped, caught his breath, and continued walking. This had happened to Martin quite a lot recently, and what he sprayed on the walls frequently frightened him. He never used such long words before; it was as if this work was done by another individual.

Martin quickly ignored the ridiculous thoughts in his mind and began jogging. He considered not attending school at all now that he was so late, but he recalled that everyone would be present today because they were expecting a new English teacher after Ms. Newe resigned. The class had to determine if this new teacher was a walk-over or not – find their vulnerable spot. The easier to bully a teacher, the more orders that the entire class should attend.

"Better collect some rocks," Martin muttered aloud, "to be prepared."

Fiona O'Malley

THE CLOSED WINDOW

Tullamore Writing Group
17 years old
Short Story

U bertha Thompson looked out the dining room sash windows and down onto an arrangement of winding, low holly bushes that connected to form a prominent T in the green grounds below. A steel grey moth fluttered by in short, staccato beats and rested on the red velvet curtains. Ubertha's slender hand tightened around her fan and beat the curtain, causing dust to rise and crushing the tiny skeleton of the moth. This swift movement caused the three inch scar below her rib cage to stretch. Ubertha gasped and clutched her side. Two weeks previously, she had had her floating ribs removed to fit more comfortably into the unmerciful corsets her mother often told her were essential for an attractive appearance.

"Carriage and poise will attract the handsomest boys," her mother would say.

And she was right. All of her mother's teachings paid off She and Ubertha's governess had moulded Ubertha into an agreeable, delightful young woman pursued by many men. The problem was that although many men secretly classified her as capable of enchanting them, she had no interest in someone with an infatuation. Although she had captured the interest of many hearts, none had captured hers.

With the exception of Mr. John Clarke.

He was a man of good connections, of humorous tales and of manners that appealed to Ubertha, but not to her father, William Thompson. Mr. Clarke and Ubertha's father disagreed on many things, primarily on politics and the state of the country. This disagreement was concluded one night when Mr. Thompson suggested that Mr. Clarke was against everything that the English government stood for.

"That, sir, is hypocrisy!" Mr. Clarke said. "I have served in her majesty's army! Your paranoia amuses me!"

"Paranoid? You think me paranoid? My suspicions are well founded!" Mr. Thompson replied.

Ubertha looked up at the roses in full bloom on the Georgian ceiling and sighed. A group of people shuffled along the floorboards. Ubertha frowned heavily. She hated Sundays. The house was open to visitors and tourists all day. A small man with a tailed waistcoat pointed at the thick walls.

"This, of course is the gothic style," the guide said, and then gestured lazily at the arched doorway, "and this, of course is the baroque style... but I often say if it's not baroque, don't fix it!"

The man chuckled to himself. Ubertha scowled. Someone coughed behind her. Ubertha spun around to face their head butler, an old man with wispy, white hair.

"What is it, George?" Ubertha said.

"It is my duty, Madame, to inform you that the lavatories downstairs are temporarily out of bounds."

"Why?"

"Well, they are presently clogged"

"Where do you suggest I relieve myself? I shall have to use them quite soon!"

"I beg you not to, the initial sight is, I assure you, quite revolting!"

"What? Is it a floater?"

George looked stunned. He opened and closed his mouth, before shuffling over to the door, muttering about an urgent message he had to deliver to the gardener.

Ubertha smiled with intense satisfaction. She loved doing that, overstepping the boundaries between what was appropriate and what was not. She loved seeing the reaction of people whenever she said something unexpected or improper. She was the one with the power to reverse things from normal to unusual. It gave her a thrill. Almost the same thrill she got from awkward silences or stubborn disagreements.

A heavy pine door to her left creaked. She turned her head and saw the square figure of her father step into the room. There was a cold silence in the air, broken by the swift footsteps of William Thompson.

He walked over to the portrait of Ubertha and her mother. A single tear rolled down his sharp cheek bone as he looked at the high ceiling and shook his head. He jumped across certain floorboards, almost as though there were invisible cracks or holes in the ground.

At the foot of the portrait and stopped and looked up. Ubertha watched her father, her face tense with anticipation. As his shoulders shook, Ubertha bit her lip.

Hard droplets of rain stabbed the soggy grass outside. Men in military uniforms ran along a pebbled footpath, looking up at the handsome face of a wrecked mansion. The roof was collapsed in the centre and the wooden windows were black and burnt. There was a light smoke rising from it, like incense.

"We must be quick!" said one of them, "there may be a second shooting soon!"

Ubertha frowned heavily. It was her mother. She must have told her father of Uberha's intensions. There was no other explanation for his dramatic reaction. Ubertha closed her eyes and took a deep breath.

"Father, it would be better if you looked at me, I have something important I wish to tell you."

Her father continued looking up at the portraits. He remained silent. Ubertha's leg began to shake and her mouth felt dry.

"I know you think I'm rash and somewhat naive, but my decision is absolute."

Mr. Thompson didn't take his eyes off the picture. Ubertha sighed.

"Mr. Clarke's feelings reflect my own for him. I intend to marry him, father, but I would engage in this matrimony with a better conscience if we had your blessing. Will you not even look at me? I know you think him unworthy, but I beg you to understand that his intensions are pure. Perhaps you are too alike, perhaps that is why your initial opinion of him is poor. I suspect you may see traits in him you dislike in yourself, but if you come to know him, you should realise that his positive characteristics outweigh the negative ones."

Mr. Thompson spun around and looked at Ubertha. Her heart sank. It was almost as though he was looking through her. He shook his head and began crying once more. Ubertha's stomach felt as though it had done a back-flip.

"Is that your answer? Will you not reconsider?" she asked.

Mr.Thompson gazed once more at the portraits and shook his head.

"What, my darlings, has become of you?" he whispered. "How has this occurred?"

Suddenly, the door opened and John Clarke strode in. Ubertha's face broke into a weak smile. She felt secure, knowing that Mr. Clarke was a very persuasive man. She was confident that everything would be alright.

John walked across to Mr. Thompson, stepping over certain floorboards on his way. A feeble ray of light shone on John's tense face. It was shiny with sweat and tears.

"Mr. Thompson," he said loudly. "We must leave now, it is not safe here!"

Ubertha's freckled forehead creased in a frown. She was sure that this was John's idea of trying to talk to her father alone, but she didn't want to be excluded from the conversation. Her father looked at John and took a deep breath.

"Maybe they're not all...."

"They are, sir," said John. "You read the letter, everyone was in the building at the time. I ask you not to think of it yet, we must go!"

John took Mr. Thompson firmly by the elbow and steered him towards the door. Ubertha scowled and walked swiftly after them.

"Mr. Clarke, I, too would like to engage in this conversation!" she said.

Mr. Clarke ignored her.

"I pray for patience, give me a shred of dignity and acknowledge my mere presence! It would be unwise, my dear, to cause any more disruption today!"

Ubertha's dress caught in an uneven floor board, but she didn't notice. The sequence on the hem began to rapidly unravel until it went rigid. Ubertha's leather boot stepped over the front of her dress and she tripped. She fell forward, and realised that she would knock into Mr. Clarke and her father. She closed her eyes as her left shoulder landed on Mr. Clarke's right one, but she didn't stop falling. She fell through Mr. Clarke's frame like air. As she finally hit the cold, wooden floor, she gasped.

Nobody heard her.

Jean Clarke

STEPHEN

Tullamore Writing Group
15 years old
Short Story

I have to brush the hair out of your eyes, those beautiful, green eyes. You're always letting your hair fall into your eyes, but I see now your eyes are closing. I see you trying to keep them open but your eyelids are too heavy. Oh, how I love your eyes. Such beautiful eyes. You're shaking. I would get you a blanket, but I don't think I can leave you, for even just a second, because I've dreamed of this. To have you here in my arms. It's all I've ever wanted since the very first day I saw you, that seems so long ago now...

I stared at the back of your head, at your dirty blonde hair, longish and messy and I loved it. I saw you doodling on the page in front of you. I wondered what you were scribbling. Then you dropped your pen, it rolled to the side of my desk. I picked it up and handed it to you. I felt your fingers against mine, they were so soft. I looked up and stared into those beautiful green eyes of yours.

You cleared your throat, my heart sped up, you were about to speak to me.

"Can I have my pen back now?" you asked, then laughed.

The girl sitting in the seat next to you, Jane Grisham, laughed too. Well, it was more of a giggle. I saw the way she looked at you just then, and I almost drove the pen into her eye to make her stop. Then I saw the look she gave me, it was a look that told me to back off. So I glared back at her. You were mine, Stephen, there was no way I was going to let a little slut like her scare me off. She seemed a bit startled by my glare.

"Freak," she muttered at me under her breath.

"Ahem."

I felt myself blush. My cheeks were burning. Oh god, I handed you the pen and letting go of that was the hardest thing I ever had to do, well back then anyway. I couldn't look you in the eye for about a week after. I was so embarrassed. I almost killed myself thinking about it over and over and over and over, until I couldn't think anymore and I didn't know what to do, so I just got up off the couch one night and walked into the bathroom. I stared at myself in the mirror for about twenty minutes, well that's how long it seemed, but I don't really know anymore.

I just stared.

I stared past the mirror and beyond that I could see you, you and that bitch, Jane Grisham. Her skirt rising far above what people regarded as respectable. Her brown hair lying softly on her shoulders, her blue eyes looking coolly into yours, her body pressed up against you, her head tilted slightly to the right and yours to the left and slowly she moves into you and your lips meet.

I screamed.

My hands rose and pulled at tufts of my hair, but I didn't cry. I hope you know that I never cried. I walked into the kitchen to find Dad standing there at the table.

"Emily, what's going on? We *have* to talk, something's going on and I can't help you if I don't know what's wrong. Tell me, please."

His voice was strong and calm. He just made me angry. How could he expect me to tell him? He leaves me here, in this goddamn house every day, he makes no effort to speak to me and now he expects me to confide in him. No, I thought, this is a joke.

"I'm FINE!"

"Do NOT raise your voice at me!"

I stared at him for a moment, and then stormed up to my room. I could hear him from downstairs, calling me back. I just kept walking, then locked the door. I searched under my bed, in my dresser, under my pillow but I couldn't find it anywhere. Did he find it? Does dad know? No, he can't, he would have said something, he would have. Then I saw it, lying on the floor where I had last left it without even thinking.

A little shard of glass.

I picked it up in my right hand and buried it into my left arm. The blood trickled out of the wound. I needed that one. I felt like I could breathe again. I dug it in once more to open a fresh wound, just to be sure. I grabbed a few wipes from my desk and cleaned myself up. Then I lay on my bed for a while. It seemed like forever, until I fell asleep. I guess that night did me good because I could think again, and that was when I made my decision.

I knew what I had to do.

I sat on the swing, just waiting, I knew it wouldn't be too long but I was feeling restless. Then I saw it. Her parents' car leaving. Their whore of a daughter wasn't with them. She had stayed at home. I walked slowly, just in case they decided to come back. That would be a very messy business indeed. Your house was just two doors down from number 47 but that was not where I was headed. I stood there for a while, just looking at it. A big two storey house. White. It was nice.

I walked on.

I knew what I had to do. I had no other choice. This was the only way that we could be together.

This would be a very messy business indeed.

Erin Tormey

FAT

Kilbeggan Writing Group
16 years old
Chapter one of her novel Fat

"**O**h my God, what an unbelievable loser. Look at her! Look at her fat ass jiggle when she walks!"

"Ew. No, I don't wanna think about her, let alone look at her! She's so gross."

Giggles erupted all around the table. Lara glanced over at the subject of their ridicule. A small, curly brown-haired girl sat alone, awkwardly poking at her food. She wore a pained expression on her face and looked as though the world owed her something. The childlike victim glanced up, catching Lara's eye. Lara flashed an uncomfortable smile which seemed to catch the girl totally off guard.

All of Lara's friends were focused on the girl, but Lara's gaze had moved and she was now transfixed on the meal that the girl was attacking with her fork. She longed to taste the creamy mashed potato and feel the butter melt in her mouth. She could almost taste the piping hot pizza that accompanied it. Lara watched the pizza as though it was about to run away and observed the steam rising from the cheese dripping from the sides. Lara felt as though if she did not eat it at that moment, she might drop dead. Her eyes lifted to the girl who cradled the object of her desire.

No, thought Lara, I'll end up like her. And I don't want to look like Kolossal Kate.

Kate shuddered as she heard the high pitch cackles of the surrounding girls. She knew why they were laughing. And it wasn't because she had done anything extraordinary, or peculiar, or funny, or anything that could possibly draw attention to her. She lowered her head and stabbed at her food with her fork, as though somehow, hurting her food would make her feel better. She looked up and saw the sea of vicious eyes examining her every move. One pair of eyes however did not seem to threaten her. They belonged to a striking blonde girl Kate had seen around the place. Lara, they called her. She wore a psychotic smile on her face that startled Kate.

Why in the name of God is she looking at me like that? Kate thought to herself, deciding to avoid their stares and dive into her food. Kate quickly devoured the meal as though it was the first thing she had eaten in days, thinking about anything but the nearby pack of ferocious hyenas. She threw her thoughts into the food that she was eating; it was far less threatening than those girls. At least her mashed potato couldn't fight back. Kate raised her head to see a tall shadow standing over her. She was astonished at what happened next.

"What does it taste like?"

It was Lara.

"Ya what?" Kate spluttered.

Lara sat down.

"Your food. What does it taste like?"

"Are you taking the piss?" Kate asked.

Lara laughed, suddenly realising how odd her question must have seemed. She had never spoken to Kolossal Kate in her life. But Lara wanted to know how the food tasted, how it felt to eat it, then maybe she wouldn't crave it quite as much. And fat Kate didn't seem to mind eating food.

"I'm sorry," Lara apologised. "I'm not making fun of you, but I need to know, what does it taste like?"

Kate paused, taking a mouthful of the mashed potato.

"Eh... mashed potato?" she replied.

Lara sighed. That was no use to her. She knew that already.

"But, what does mashed potato taste like? How does it feel?"

Kate looked totally baffled.

"Well, to be honest, this stuff tastes like shite. But my Dad's mashed potato is to die for."

To die for.

Lara wondered if food could actually be worth dying for.

"What does his taste like? Describe it to me."

Kate smiled. Her deep, brown, almond shaped eyes shone as though she had just received the best news ever. Looking at her, Lara realised that

Kate was actually quite pretty. She was just hiding behind the frumpy clothes, frizzy hair and large glasses. For the first time, Lara realised that Kate was a human being. She had feelings, just like Lara, and contrary to Lara's friends' beliefs, she was more than just a fat ass.

"It's creamy and smooth, kind of milky and..."

Lara stopped Kate short.

"I'm sorry. I never introduced myself. I'm Lara."

Kate smiled, pretending this was news to her.

"I'm Kate," she replied, blushing.

"Anyway, go on," Lara said.

Kate stared awkwardly at her food, suddenly realising she had been going on about her father's stupid mashed potatoes to the most popular girl in the whole school. Lara doesn't care about mashed potatoes, she thought. She cares about boys, and parties, and makeup, not about some loser's father's mashed potatoes.

Oh God, thought Kate. She must think I'm totally insane.

Kate quickly tried to come up with an excuse, anything to get her away from Lara.

"I... eh... I've got to..."

Kate leapt up from her seat and made her way rapidly to the bathroom.

"Kate!" Lara called after her.

Oh God, I've scared her off, thought Lara.

Lara contemplated whether or not to follow her.

"No... I've bothered her enough for one day."

She returned to the table where her friends sat. They all stared at her, jaws dropped. It suddenly dawned on Lara what she had just done. This would not be good for her reputation.

"What a loser," she sighed as she sat down.

"OMG!" shrieked Ebony, a loud-mouthed girl, with crimson streaks in her hair.

"I can't believe you actually talked to her! What did you say?"

Lara felt a pang of guilt at the bottom of her stomach. She had just given them another reason to laugh at poor Kate.

"Oh... I just, eh... invited her to a party tonight," stuttered Lara.

A collective gasp was heard all around the table.

"You did what?" squealed Ebony. "Are your parents going away again?"

Lara smiled. "No. But then... there is *no* party...." Lara's grin widened.

"Nice one," Ebony smiled. "Fatty doesn't know there's no party!"

"Ooh... Burn."

The girls laughed simultaneously.

Kate sat in the grimy bathroom stall. She curled up into a ball and clutched her knees, rocking back and forth as the tears streamed silently down her face. Humiliated once more.

What have I done to deserve this? she asked herself.

She spent her days avoiding girls like Lara. She deliberately tried to blend in, anything to steer clear of their attention. But her efforts obviously weren't good enough. She would never fit in. She would always have to hide away.

Kate sat slumped against the rickety wall of the cramped bathroom stall, wishing the toilet would just swallow her up. How could she be stupid enough to believe that Lara Matthews was actually interested in talking to her?

Kate jumped when she heard the creaky door to the toilets swing open. She lifted her knees closer to her, hoping that whoever it was wouldn't think that there was anyone in there. She was already late for class, and it would probably be Mrs. Elliot, shooing all the stragglers to lessons. She held her breath and listened to the heels clacking along the tiles. The clacking stopped, and Kate looked down to see a pair of red stilettos standing outside her stall.

Lara paused outside the door that was adorned with years and years of graffiti with her hand raised, ready to knock. What was she going to say? How could she possibly explain herself?

"Kate?" she said quietly.

Silence.

"Kate, it's me, Lara."

From behind the door she heard a sniffle.

"Go away."

Lara paused, unsure of her next move. This girl was her only hope of resisting temptation. She couldn't do this on her own anymore.

"Kate, please, come out. I was just hoping we could be friends..."

Lara spoke softly. She could hear Kate sobbing quietly inside the stall.

"Friends?" replied Kate. "Leave me alone. Girls like you don't want to be friends with girls like me. You have everyone else in the whole goddamn school on your side. You're everyone's friend! You don't want me. I'm not stupid, I know."

"Kate," Lara interrupted, "please just come out."

She thought for a few moments. Kate was right. Girls like Lara and girls like Kate didn't mix. But she had to convince Kate otherwise.

"Kate, honestly, I just want to talk."

The door swung open almost hitting Lara in the face. Kate stepped out. She stood facing Lara, her face red, her eyes puffy.

"So talk," she said sternly.

Kate looked up at Lara. She was about a foot taller than Kate.

"Look, Kate," Lara said softly. "I just think we should be friends, that's all."

Kate was growing more and more angry. Did Lara seriously think she believed her?

"Friends?" Kate screeched. "Lara! You've lived across the road from me for over thirteen years! You're in almost all of my classes! You see me every day at lunchtime! And never once have you even spoken to me, let alone tried to be my friend! And now you want to be my friend?!"

Kate could feel her heart almost bursting from her chest; her body began to tingle from the sudden surge of heat.

Lara sighed.

"Kate, I know, I know. It's just, I'm so sick of girls like Ebony and Ashlie and all those other girls! All they talk about is boys and bitching and themselves. They don't care about anyone else. I can't take it anymore. I need to be friends with an actual human being for once. One who isn't totally insane. And I just thought we could..."

Kate studied Lara's chiseled face.

Was she being serious?

It makes sense, Kate thought to herself. I could never be friends with that loudmouth, Ebony. Maybe she's telling the truth.

"So why me?" Kate asked somberly.

Lara looked down at Kate and smiled to herself. She was buying it.

"Why you?" she asked. "Because, Kate, you're different to those girls. I've seen you around, you seem nice. And you're a smart girl. It would be nice to have some intelligent company, rather than these brainless idiots with their one-track minds."

Kate looked down at her shoes uncomfortably.

I'm in, thought Lara smugly.

"Look, I understand if you don't want to but..."

Kate interrupted Lara quickly.

"No, no! You're right. We should be friends."

Lara held out her hand.

"Friends?" she asked.

Kate grasped her hand tightly with her own sweaty hand.

"Friends," she whispered quietly.

Dorothy Jozefecka

CLOCKWORK

Kilbeggan Writing Group
15 years old
Short Story

Tears sprung into Megan's eyes as she listened to her own quick footsteps on the pavement. She couldn't believe her parents were fighting again. She couldn't even remember what they were fighting about. Megan could still hear her mother's loud shrieks as she walked through the creeping shadows, further away from the house.

Megan knew this town too well to be freaked out by a few shadows.

Moving into a quiet, sleepy street, Megan slowed her pace. Yells from the other block were no longer in the air, and once again, Megan could breathe deeply.

"Why the hell do they do this?" she muttered to herself, her footsteps echoing around her.

A loud bark from one of the walled gardens was the only response to Megan's question. Closing her eyes for a second, Megan tried to think of a place where she could take shelter for few hours, just long enough to let things at home calm down. Opening her eyes again, she glanced at the white face of her watch.

"A quarter past nine. It's too early," Megan muttered.

A grunt escaped her mouth as she looked around. She had blindly walked down a narrow alley at the back of a tall, abandoned building. Megan could feel a shiver building up on the back of her neck as she glanced at the cold, old walls, which were decorated with graffiti and urine. Taking her eyes off of the building, Megan watched her breath turn into a white cloud in front of her face.

"Shit," she cursed silently and rubbed her hands together. "I hate November."

Looking at her watch again, Megan exhaled the cold air from her lungs.

Quarter past nine.

"Is this stupid thing broken?"

She pressed the face of the watch to her ear and flinched slightly as the cold plastic cover touched her skin. Loud ticking filled Megan's head and she blinked, confused.

"To hell with this."

She shoved her hands into her jacket pockets and moved towards the other side of the alley, where the street lamps shone so dimly they might as well be off The sound of her footsteps was strangely magnified, the air above her echoed like a marching army. Megan stood still, cautiously looked around, certain that someone would appear out of nowhere to give out to her for disturbing the silence. Just as she was about to start walking again, the air filled again with the sound of more footsteps – someone else's footsteps.

"Shit."

Megan's stomach tightened and she shivered. She couldn't get caught here. This was certainly no place for a teenage girl to be hanging around after dark. Images of drugs and violence flooded Megan's mind and the only escape route open to her was a bad choice. It was too far to try to run towards the next street. She would have to hide in the entrance to the derelict building that loomed so dark in front of her.

The footsteps behind Megan didn't change pace as she cautiously moved towards the broken double doors. One side was barely holding on its hinges. With every step Megan took, the other person was getting closer. She didn't dare to look back at the alley before the total darkness of the old house swallowed her. She slipped through the collapsed door, her heart racing.

The stench of rotting furniture and damp wallpaper filled Megan's nostrils, making her gag. Her eyes watered as she forced her stomach to calm down. Blinking away the burning tears, she moved further into the house. Megan's eyes slowly adjusted to the surrounding darkness. Contours of walls and old furniture came into focus as, with every step, she moved deeper into the haunted house – at least, that's what she used to think of this place when she was little.

The footsteps in the alley stopped.

Oh god, Megan thought, knowing that whoever had been walking down the alley was now standing still. Watching. Waiting.

Something crossed her unsteady path and Megan clasped her hands over her mouth to muffle the sound of the shriek that escaped her half open lips.

Rats!

Megan breathed through her fingers.

She could hear the sound of her heart beating, and silently wondered if anyone else would be able to hear it in the complete silence that rolled over every inch of space.

Pulling her hands away from her mouth, Megan swallowed and took another step forward. She wished she could go back and run towards that dimly lit street. She would do anything to be back outside where semi-fresh air replaced the sickly sweet taste of dampness.

Megan swallowed hard and flinched slightly as she forced her tongue to gather more moisture from her dry mouth. She reached the entrance of another corridor.

This is a maze, Megan thought, exhaling and looking around the hallway opening in front of her. To her surprise, the door at the end of this lesser corridor was surrounded by a thin stream of light. The room behind the door was lit up.

Someone else was in the building.

Probably some homeless person.

Megan held her breath. A quick look behind assured Megan that whoever was outside had not followed her into the house. Whoever it was, they probably hadn't the courage to come in. Right then, Megan wanted to leave this God-forsaken place. Leave, or at least stay in one place where no one can see you, she told herself.

I could peek through the keyhole, she thought, and even though she could barely hear her own footsteps over the sound of her heartbeat, Megan continued down the hallway towards the light. She noticed it was flickering slightly.

Candlelight, she thought, noiselessly mouthing the words in unison with her thoughts. Each cautious step on the gritty carpet brought her closer to the door. The smell of dampness was slowly retracting, only to be replaced by the even more overpowering smell of, what Megan assumed was, incense.

It took forever to arrive at the door. Megan looked down to see the golden light flicker around her runners. Instead of looking in the key hole like she had planned, she felt compelled to go through the door. She reached out her hand and rested it on the freezing cold of the brass doorknob. The surface of the doorknob seamed to curve into Megan's hand, making her fingers lock tighter around it.

The sound of distant footsteps echoed softly behind Megan.

"Hell no," she moaned softly, realising that her stalker was following her into the house.

Another curse escaped Megan's mouth as she turned the doorknob and pushed the heavy door open. A stream of light flooded into the hallway, half blinding

Megan, whose eyes had already adapted to the house's everlasting darkness. The smell of incense hit her like a slap in the face, catching in her throat. Megan heard a sudden shriek; it came from her mystery predator, somewhere in the blackness of the house. Megan quickly forced herself into the light and closed the door behind her.

Her eyes stung from the glaring candle light. But someone else was in the room with her. It was a man. He was moving fast, his hands darting over candles and incense sticks, trying to put them out.

Megan's terrified gaze fell over the man, who turned to face her, a look of utter surprise and disbelief on his face.

Megan's heart stopped, she could no longer feel its beat, could no longer hear the blood pulsing through her ears. What felt like a bucket of ice cold water washed over Megan's stomach as she stumbled back to the door.

The man rushed towards her, his arms outstretched. Megan wanted to scream, but she could barely breathe. The man's hands locked around Megan's shoulder, his claw like fingers digging deep into her skin.

"You shouldn't be here," he hissed, exposing his yellowing teeth. "Not yet."

He shook Megan, and after a second let her go, rushing to put out the countless candles that filled the room.

Megan still couldn't bring herself to speak, or move. She looked at the man, who seemed absolutely insane, not only in his actions, but also in his appearance. His long forearms were nearly entirely covered in watches. His outfit looked as if it was put together by a blind person. The man would have been completely bald, if it wasn't for the ponytail of curly orange hair, which grew out of the back of his head.

Megan reached for the doorknob, hoping she could escape, both from this madman, and from whoever was in the hallway behind her.

"Don't you dare move," the man hissed, half running towards her.

He pushed Megan out of his way, leaned heavily against the door, and turned the key which was in the lock.

Somehow, the man managed to put out all of the candles and seconds later footsteps could be heard on the other side of the door. Megan pushed her back to the wall, wishing it could open and let her escape from the choking smell of incense. She swallowed, trying to keep the taste of bile from her mouth. The footsteps drew closer and closer. Megan held her breath, clenching her teeth when the sound of the doorknob turning filled the air.

The door rattled.

White spots flooded Megan's vision as she pressed her head against the cold wall.

They can't get in, she comforted herself.

The man moved to Megan's right. Megan couldn't take it. She parted her lips to scream for help. A calloused hand quickly clasped over her mouth. Ticking of watches filled her head and Megan froze.

"Don't move," he hissed, the smell of garlic and unwashed mouth coming together with the warning. "It's you behind you and you can't meet you."

Megan had no idea what he was saying. She didn't dare move a muscle. The footsteps slowly receded away from the door and with every fading step the man lessened the pressure over Megan's mouth.

He took his hand away when the sound finally died.

"You shouldn't be here," he repeated, and Megan could feel him walking away in the darkness.

She didn't respond.

"This has ruined everything..." he muttered to himself.

Megan side stepped in the direction of the locked door. If the key was still in the lock, she could have a chance of escaping.

"Don't go yet. There's too much risk," the man said harshly from the black.

Megan's gaze turned towards the source of the sound. Suddenly, a spark appeared and the crazy man re-lit a candle.

"Risk of what?" Megan managed to say, her voice trembling.

In the dim light of a single candle Megan could feel her stomach unclenching.

"Risk of a collision."

The man's yellowing teeth seemed almost golden in the light.

"Go to hell," Megan muttered and moved towards the door.

"Don't! You're not ready yet!"

The man's hand flew into the air, signalling to her to stop.

"Not ready for what?"

Hot blood rushed into Megan's head and she stopped, afraid that if she took one more step, she would fall.

Thinking that he had won the argument, the man lowered his hand.

"Not ready to see yourself."

His voice filled with an all-knowing tone.

Megan didn't have the time, or the will, to stay in the room. She just wanted to go home. She wanted to go back to her mother's shrieks and her father's threats. Most of all, Megan wanted to leave the madman here, to rot like the rest of the house.

"I see myself everyday in the mirror," she said. "I have no problem seeing myself."

With a few more steps, Megan reached the door and turned the key, grateful to hear the sound of the lock opening.

To Megan's surprise, the man didn't move to stop her. Megan opened the door, ready to run back the way she came, ready to push this unpleasant experience to the back of her mind.

"My name is Nigel... Remember that," the man said.

Megan turned to give him one more look. He blew out the candle.

Darkness fell upon Megan's tired body for the third time this evening. She didn't wait. Instead she rushed through the hallways as quickly as she could, no longer cautious about making too much noise. She ran down the front steps of the house and kept running until she reached the street she'd walked down earlier. Not looking back, Megan hurried towards her house.

"I don't believe it," Megan muttered, looking down at her watch.

It was nearly midnight.

Slowing down to a brisk walk, Megan was surprised to hear other footsteps in the street. Stopping under a tree she looked around, worried that she might have been followed.

It took Megan a few seconds to realise that the footsteps were in front of her, not behind. Quickly passing the neighbours' houses, she walked into the alley leading to her house.

Megan stopped.

At the end of the alley she saw a black haired girl, turning a corner in the direction of her home. A profile view of the girl nearly knocked Megan to the ground. Even from this far away Megan was more than sure she recognised everything about the girl, from her navy jacket to her watery blue eyes.

It was her. It was Megan. Another Megan!

Tears stung Megan's eyes as Nigel's voice echoed in her head.

"Not ready to see yourself..."

This couldn't be true.

Megan's legs carried her forward, towards her house. From the shadows of the alley, she watched the other girl climbing the drainpipe and disappearing through the open window of her *own* bedroom – the bedroom window that Megan had left open earlier tonight.

"It isn't true. It can't be." Megan exclaimed, her voice stirring the sleepy silence.

Images of her parents fighting flooded Megan's mind, only to be followed by a vision of the madman named Nigel.

"What the hell is going on? Nigel, he did something to me. He must have! He must have drugged me. The incense smoke, it has to be. What the hell was that stuff?"

But all the reassuring arguments made no difference. Megan gagged and doubled over as her undigested dinner spilled on the pavement, splattering pieces of carrot on her trousers and runners.

"It isn't true."

Megan wiped her mouth, the taste of stomach acid lingering on her tongue.

She hurried towards her house and skilfully climbed the drainpipe until she got hold of the windowsill. Inside, the room was empty. Her lamp glowed warmly and everything was just as Megan had left it a few hours before.

She grunted and closed the window behind her, breathing a sigh of relief.

"I'm not going mad. I'm fine," she repeated over and over to herself.

Megan sat on the edge of her bed.

She glanced down at her watch, and instantly her heart was thundering in her ears again.

The second hand moved.

Nine fifteen.

What the hell was going on?

David O'Shea

A QUIET EXIISTENCE

Tullamore Writing Group
16 years old
Chapter three of his novel

– 11:23pm, 25th May 2006 –

Grace Plant sat in her small room. She stared out the barred window at the cloudy night sky. Tears rolled slowly down her face. On the bed beside her was a complete stranger, a woman she had met just 2 hours ago, named Dani. A car drove by, its headlights illuminating the dark sign just outside her window. *Lexington Mental Asylum.* The words were swept into darkness again as the car left. Grace began to sob harder than ever, remembering how she had ended up in this strange, scary hospital in the first place...

❧

"OK, OK Mom, but this better be good. I had plans for today, you know? When do you want me to come over?"

Grace spoke angrily to her mother on the phone. It was 8:00am on a cold, Sunday morning. Grace's mother had called her, insisting she come by straight away. Apparently, there was something incredibly important she needed to talk to Grace about.

"Can you get here as soon as possible Grace? Please, this is very important."

"Alright, but the quickest I'll be there is about an hour. Can I bring Tom?" Grace asked.

There was a very long pause.

Finally her mother replied, "OK, see you about nine."

Tom was Grace's boyfriend. They had met 6 months ago, beside the lake in the park. It was love at first sight for both of them. Tom was everything Grace had ever wanted. He was a tall, broad man with jet-black hair – very handsome. Grace had introduced Tom to her parents for the first time last week. She remembered how nervous Tom had been about meeting them. The odd thing was that when Grace had introduced him to her parents, they had seemed more worried than he had. In fact, now that she thought of it, all her mom and dad had said was hello and goodbye.

Grace wanted to change that, give them another chance to get to know her true love. Maybe there'd be more conversation between Tom and her parents today? Grace reached towards the phone again to call Tom. Suddenly, it rang again.

"Hello?" Grace said into the phone.

"Hey, baby!"

It was Tom. The very sound of his voice made Grace's heart melt.

"Tom! Hi! I was just about to call you! Wow, that is so weird. How are you?"

"Hmmm... Well let's see... I'm in love with the greatest person in the world, so how do you think I am?"

"Oh really? Well, who's the lucky girl, Tom?" Grace asked, laughing. Tom chuckled.

"So, Gracey, are we still going to the park today?"

"Aw Tom, I'm so sorry, but my Mom asked me to go over to her house, said she needed to talk about something really important. Will you come with me? We'll go to the park afterwards. How does that sound?"

"That sounds great," Tom replied.

They arranged for Grace to pick Tom up outside his apartment in the middle of town, and go to her parent's house from there. After Grace hung up, she got dressed. She stared into the mirror, and a beautiful, green-eyed, slim, red-haired nineteen year old girl stared back at her.

Grace left her apartment at 8:30 and hopped into her Volkswagen Golf. When she turned the key in the ignition, the radio came on. Grace checked the radio volume was at an even number, one of her obsessive compulsive disorder traits. She took off for the city.

Five minutes later, she pulled up at the Sunrise Apartments. As planned, Tom was waiting outside for her. He smiled as the car pulled up beside him. One thing Grace loved about Tom was that he was never late. He always showed up at the right place at the right time. Grace jumped out of the car and flung her arms around Tom's neck. He kissed her tenderly. An old woman, who was walking by, gave them a very odd look. Grace just smiled.

There's nothing wrong with public displays of affection if you're in love, she thought.

"It's so good to see you!" Tom said, still smiling. "You look amazing, as always."

"Well, you don't look so bad yourself!" Grace beamed up at him.

They arrived at Grace's parent's house, as she had planned, at exactly 9:00. Grace was very rarely wrong about times. She *had* to have a time planned out for everything, just another one of the things she obsessed about. Grace drove up the long driveway, towards the house she had grown up in. She went to park in her usual parking space outside the house, but found it was occupied by a large, black van.

That's strange, Grace thought, pulling up beside the van.

Grace and Tom walked up to the door hand in hand and she rang the doorbell. Her Dad opened the door. Grace let go of Tom's hand and threw her arms around her father.

"Hey, Daddy!" she smiled.

Her father hugged her back, but it was a very lifeless, weak hug, very unlike the strong, comforting ones he usually gave. Grace stopped hugging him. Something was wrong. She had never seen him look so worried.

"Daddy... What is it?" she asked, suddenly very worried.

"I'll explain in a minute, Grace. Could you come into the living room please?"

Grace glanced over at Tom. He looked just as confused and worried as she did.

"Um... Grace... Mr. Plant... Would it be OK if I used the bathroom?" Tom asked nervously.

Mr. Plant didn't say anything. He kept looking at Grace with those worried eyes.

"Sure, go ahead Tom..." Grace answered, turning to look at her handsome boyfriend.

That's when Mr. Plant looked at Tom for the first time. When he glanced back at Grace he looked more worried than before. As Tom walked up the stairs, Grace followed her father into the sitting room.

Her mother was sitting on the couch. She was sobbing slightly, holding a tissue to her eyes.

"Mom?" Grace whispered.

There were two other people in the room. Both were tall men, wearing white uniforms. Spread across the left breast of their jackets were the three words Grace would come to cry about. *Lexington Mental Asylum*.

"Mom... Dad... What's going on?" Grace asked weakly.

"I think I can answer that," one of the men in the white suits said quietly.

He had blonde hair, a kind face, and a gentle voice.

"Please Grace, sit down..."

Grace sat down and searched her mother's sobbing face. But her mother wouldn't look at her.

"Grace, my name is Dr. Bowie. I'm from the Lexington Asylum in town. We want to talk to you about your partner, Tom."

"Tom? Why? What's wrong with Tom?" Grace asked confusedly.

"Is Tom here with you today, Grace?" Dr. Bowie asked her gently, sitting near her.

Grace didn't know what to say. She didn't want these strange men to take Tom away from her. She had never been happier in her life. She *needed* Tom.

"Your mother told us you were bringing Tom with you," Dr. Bowie said patiently.

Not once did he take his eyes off Grace's face. Even when she looked away, Grace could feel his eyes on her.

"Well... Um..." Grace fumbled, staring at the floor.

People had obviously heard Tom and her come in. Her dad had already seen Tom. So what could she say? Grace glanced over at her father. He looked sadly back at her. But he didn't say anything.

"Of course he's here," said Grace. "He's upstairs in the bathroom."

"You're *sure* he's here?" Dr. Bowie asked.

Grace frowned.

"Well unless he jumped out the window since he went up there."

Grace tried to smile, anything to diffuse the tension. But instead of smiling, she burst out crying. These men were here for Tom. They couldn't take him away from her – they couldn't.

"P–please!" she wailed, "*Please*! Don't take Tom away, *please*. He's perfectly normal, he's sane. He's good to me. I love him, *PLEASE*!"

Dr. Bowie patted her hand.

"Oh Grace... We're not here for Tom..." he said.

Grace stopped crying.

"You're not?" she asked, puzzled.

And suddenly she realised.

No – it wasn't possible.

"Well Grace... You see... We're here for you," Dr. Bowie replied.

Grace's mouth dropped open.

"Me? But... Why me? What's... What's wrong with *me*?" Grace asked.

Dr. Bowie sighed.

"Grace... Your partner, Tom. Well, he's... He's not real. He's all in here."

Dr. Bowie tapped the side of his head. Grace couldn't believe it.

It must be a joke, she thought. It has to be a joke.

"Tom's not real? Aw, come *on*! Mom, Dad, how could you scare me like this?" Grace exploded angrily.

"No one's joking, Grace," Dr. Bowie said. "Your parents said they've never even seen Tom before, and you introduced them to thin air just last week. Tom is just a figment of your imagination."

Grace couldn't believe what she was hearing. She refused to believe it.

"Mom, Dad, you met Tom last week, he was here! Dad, you saw him coming in, you heard him asking to use the bathroom!"

Dr. Bowie turned to his partner, a man who was silently watching everything.

"Dr. Yorke, would you kindly go upstairs and check if Tom is in the bathroom? If he is, bring him down please. Mr. and Mrs. Plant, you don't mind if Dr. Yorke goes upstairs do you?"

Mr. Plant shook his head.

"Go ahead," he said dryly.

Mrs. Plant continued to sob.

Yes, go upstairs and get Tom, Grace thought frantically, watching Dr. Yorke leave the room. You'll see he exists, and then we're leaving, me and Tom, we're going to the park for a romantic stroll. Oh God, he is real. I know he's real. He has to be real. I love him. God, I love him.

Soon, the living room door opened and Dr. Yorke entered the room alone.

"Not a soul up there, Dr. Bowie," he said, in a low, deep voice.

"I see..."

Dr. Bowie turned to Grace.

"Grace, I know this may come as a shock to you, but if you'll just come with us now, we'll bring you to the hospital, get you a nice room, and help you get *better*, OK?"

Grace wanted to explode. She shook her head slowly, but it got faster, more frantic.

A Quiet Existence · 43

"No... No, no, he *does* exist, he *has* to... I..." she began.

Then she suddenly leaped up, tears streaming from her eyes, and bolted towards the door, screaming.

"No! No. I won't go with you. He's real! Tom! *TOM!*"

She burst out of the living room towards the stairs. Someone tackled her to the ground, pinning her down. It was Dr. Yorke. He was very strong, and as Grace struggled to get out of his tight grip, Dr. Bowie appeared above her, holding a large syringe. He injected it into her neck. Suddenly, Grace's heart beats began to slow. She felt relaxed. She looked around and saw her mother, her face buried into her father's shirt, sobbing as he held her tight, also crying.

The two men carried her out the front door, and as they brought her towards the big, black van that occupied her usual parking space, she looked up at the window of her old bedroom. Standing in the window was Tom, slamming his fist hard against the glass, screaming something she couldn't make out.

Mary Seery

DRIP

Kilbeggan Writing Group
17 years old
Short Story

D rip, drip, drip.
Laura stood at the mouth of the cave and peered down. She studied the circular entrance. The cave was about 6 foot high so she could walk upright in it. However, she couldn't even guess how deep the diagonal path was that lead down into the earth. She stepped in slowly and gasped as the icy air hit her, raising goose bumps on her uncovered arms. Her eyes strained in the dimness as she started to move carefully down the steep path. Laura turned and gave one last glance behind her. The trees all around the entrance were still. The forest stretched for miles either side of the old mine shaft.

"You can do this," she whispered to herself, looking back into the black.

Laura descended further into the mine shaft, her feet crunching over the loose pebbles, her ears listening for any other noise besides the sound of her own pounding footsteps and heavy breathing. She heard nothing, but she knew there was something in here, lurking in the dark. She had no torch or source of light besides the fading sun behind her. Laura's eyes began adjusting to the gloom and now she could make out the general shapes of the obstacles that lay in her path. She heard a scraping to her left. She spun around quickly, trying to catch a glimpse of whatever it was. Laura was both horrified and relieved to see a large rat scampering back up towards the cave entrance. Her top lip twitched, repulsed by the creature. She felt a quick shiver shooting through her, straight to the ground.

The sound of the rat faded away leaving everything silent again.

Laura continued cautiously. Suddenly she heard a moan. She paused, swallowing quietly. The groan was stretched and pained, like an animal in distress. She sucked in the moist air as fear gripped her, binding her chest.

That's no rat, she thought.

Laura's ears pricked up, straining to distinguish what the sound was. Terror gripped her heart like a vice when she heard the noise a second time. Laura raised the crowbar in front of her defensively. She wasn't going to be caught off guard again. She knew the noise was coming from deeper in the cave.

You've got to keep going, she told herself reluctantly, placing one foot before the other.

How could he do such a thing? she asked herself over and over.

Suddenly she heard the moan again, it sounded like a word. Laura knew the moan was coming from a couple of paces to her left. She was so close now. She took a deep breath and prepared herself. Besides the constant dripping she could now make out the definite sound of heavy breathing. Slowly she turned, staring intensely into the dark, trying to distinguish her target from the cold pressing walls surrounding her. She saw from the corner of her eye a lump rising from the ground. Inside, Laura felt calm as she walked over to the shape. She raised the crowbar over her head. From inside her she felt a vicious rage burst out from her core.

The cave was suddenly filled with an indistinguishable cry, a cry of fury.

Laura slammed the crowbar down on her target with a sickening crunch.

A man fell to the cave floor. Laura pounded him with everything she had, all her built up rage. She hated him completely. Finally she paused for a moment and cautiously licked her lips. A coppery, metallic taste filled her mouth. A small smile spread across her face and she continued pounding until she felt weak, until she knew the man was dead.

Laura slumped to the ground and began to sob.

She had finally done it, her first kill. The clan was going to be so proud. She dragged herself up and took a deep breath. She wasn't done yet; she still had a lot more to do. Laura rolled her shoulders and stretched out. Warily, she bent down and looped her arms under the dead man's armpits. She shuddered as she felt the body's warmth, but it was losing heat quickly. Laura tugged. The man was heavy. Slowly, she began to drag the body to the cave entrance, getting it ready for transportation. Half way there, Laura stumbled and fell. The body rolled over her legs pinning her a moment. She lay there, limbs shaking.

"Laura, Laura, where the hell are you?" a voice called urgently in the dark.

Laura was so drained that she couldn't raise her head.

"Who's there?" she called out feebly.

"It's Tony."

The voice answered much closer this time. Laura felt a hand on her shoulder. Tony, her adviser, tugged her arm and pulled her free of her burden.

"Did you do it?" he asked, panting as Laura dusted herself off

"I...I did," Laura stammered.

"It wasn't easy but after thinking about what he did to my sister, I found the strength to go through with it. I'm so thankful to the Clan for helping me track this scumbag down."

"You know that's what we do, help people with their revenge, but I... I have some bad news. The intel we received about this guy here was false."

Tony waited a few moments for the news to sink in before continuing.

"I'm so sorry, Laura, but this isn't the guy who maimed and killed your sister. If there is anything the Clan can do..."

The rest of his words were drowned off as Laura ran up to the entrance of the cave, her head spinning. Waves of remorse and regret hit her, each new one wrenching the contents of her stomach up. After she had spewed up everything in her stomach she stood in a catatonic state, her thoughts in chaos, nothing to comfort her but a constant sound of ringing terribly in her ears.

Drip. Drip. Drip.

Leona MacManus

THE DIARY OF LISA TUMULTY

Kilbeggan Writing Group
17 years old
Chapter one of her novel
The Diary of Lisa Tumulty

Jesus Christ, Drew. It's Lisa, come here, quick!"

Lisa's mother jumped up and down in the doorway as she frantically called for help.

"Hurry, there's something wrong."

Oh my God, Lisa panicked. What's happening to me? Why am I shaking like this? I can't stop it. Help! I'm dying.

Lisa's body was shaking violently as though bolts of electricity were jolting through her. Her head banged against her pillow while her right arm and leg slapped the mattress in repetitive thrusts.

I can't die, I can't. What about all my plans? I have to see James again! I have to stop it.

She desperately tried to use her free hand to restrain the other but she couldn't. It was as though her actions were being controlled by little men inside her brain, pulling switches this way and that so that she shook helplessly.

Help me, please help me.

She tried to shout for help, but she couldn't. Her mouth was being controlled so that all that would come out were incomprehensible loud grunts.

Oh my God! This is pointless. I'm going to die. So much for my big vision of the ninety year old Lisa Tumulty, falling asleep in her rocking chair and not waking up.

Through blurry vision Lisa could make out two pale faces creased with worry. Oh thank God, help has come. Wait, why are you just standing there? Hello, your only daughter is kind of dying here. Help me!

They're so useless, Lisa groaned to herself. What am I going to do? It won't stop.

She tried once again to restrain her arm. She failed.

Oh please God, make it stop, I'll do anything.

Tears rolled down Lisa's cheeks.

It's not going to stop! I'm going to shake like this forever. It's not fair. What did I ever do to deserve this? This is so cruel! Please, please, please stop.

Her body grew quiet.

Hey, it's over. Thank you, God, thank you.

"Mum. Dad," Lisa gasped, relieved at being able to speak those two simple words.

Thanks a mill for standing there watching me die. You really were a great help, she thought.

Lisa threw her legs over the bed and put her bare feet to the ground before collapsing into a heap on the floor.

Now what? she thought, panicking once more as visions of her in a wheelchair flashed before her. She tried to get up again, but failed once more.

My... my feet, they're gone! What's wrong with me? I can't get up. I need to get up. I need to.... help me. Come on feet, come on, please work, please.

She stood up.

"Oh, thank God,' she sighed.

"Are you ok, Lisa?"

Her mother linked her elbow.

"Let's go down to the kitchen."

Her dad took her other arm.

With the help of her parents, she eventually made it to the darkened kitchen.

"Sit there for a minute until we try to figure out what to do," her father said, easing Lisa's weak body onto the couch.

For a few moments her parents sat there studying her as they tried to figure out a plan.

Oh for Christ's' sake why don't they just lay me down in a coffin, Lisa thought impatiently. She couldn't bare the uneasy silence or the pitiful looks.

What was that? Lisa crinkled her forehead and studied her mother.

Now look, she's trying to come up with something. This should be good.

"It was probably a reaction to a bad nightmare," her mother finally said.

Oh please, that's the worst thing I've ever heard. A bad nightmare! Does she think I'm *that* thick?

Lisa exploded.

"Oh for Gods' sake, mum, I'm not stupid. There's something wrong with me and you know it."

Lisa's' mother put her arm around her daughter.

Oh would she ever give it a rest, Lisa thought, shoving her mother away. She's so bad at the whole comforting thing.

"Lisa, honey, what's wrong?" her mum whined, hurt. "I'm only trying to..."

Lisa cut her off

"Trying to what, Mum? Ease my worries? I'm after having a fit for Christ's sake. And you come up with the stupidest reason."

God I'm terrible, Lisa thought, but she has to learn to lay off sometimes.

"Ok, we're going straight to hospital."

Lisa's father jumped from his chair and made for the car keys lying on the windowsill. His wife grabbed his arm.

"Do you really think there's a need for that, Drew? I mean, it may have been a once off?"

Drew rolled his eyes.

Who is she trying to fool? Lisa grumbled internally. Would she ever give it a rest and admit that she's worried. What's the point in trying to calm others when your own nerves are shot?

"How do we know if it was a once off?" her father snapped. "What do we do? Sit here and wait to see if it happens again? No, we can't take any chances."

"But," his wife stuttered.

"We're going, Etna, and that's that."

Lisa's mother sighed and went out to get the coats out in the hall.

She's scared, Lisa thought, chewing worriedly on her thumb nail. Who am I kidding, I'm scared.

Five minutes later and they were on the way to the A and E.

Well this is fine communication for you, Lisa thought as she glared at the back of her parents' heads. Twenty minutes travelling and no one had said a word. Lisa's father focused on the road while her mother nervously fiddled with her fingers. Lisa sat in the back of the car, tightly hugging her old teddy for comfort.

How sad am I? It's bad when a fourteen year old had to resort to the comfort of a stuffed bear. Still, nobody else is any use, are they teddy?

Lisa's mother tapped her clicky, patented black shoes against the horrible white-washed floor. It stank of disinfectant.

"Would you stop that, you're making me anxious."

Lisa lost her patience yet again.

Could she not just keep still for God's sake? I hate this.

Lisa longed to be anywhere but here, in the pokey waiting room of her local doctor where all there was to gaze at were amputated dolls and out of date magazines. Could they not find any better furniture than these musty, maroon coloured couches? They look like they were bought in a junk sale?

Lisa looked at the clock.

Four o'clock. So much for catering for emergencies, we've been waiting for over an hour. Lucky I'm not on my deathbed, because this would suck.

Just as Lisa was planning a school debate on the horrible state of hospitals, a tall dark man in a white coat approached them.

"We can see you now, sorry for the delay. I'm Doctor O'Loughlin."

He grinned as though it were a pleasant thing to see a teenage girl with a pale face and matted hair, sitting upon one of his big, manky couches at four in the morning.

You suck.

Lisa knew she was desperate for judging people but she couldn't help it, already she didn't like Doctor O'Loughlin. There was something in his cheeky smile that hinted he was smirking at his own private joke. He brought them into his room and put them sitting on black leather chairs. At least they were a little more comfortable than the dreaded couches.

"Now, what seems to be the problem?" asked Doctor O'Loughlin, studying Lisa's parents' worried expressions.

Her mother launched into a big detailed description of the night.

Oh my God, was it really like that? Lisa wondered.

Her mother described Lisa's fit.

"She was convulsing, thrashing about, her head banging the pillow."

Lisa glanced at the doctor. He looked miles away. Lisa felt like saying, Wake-y, wake-y. Sure, mum's a bit of a head case at times and difficult to listen to, but Mr. Suck-y doctor, you could show a bit of interest with an odd nod or a smile. Is she that boring that you have to daydream, or night dream, or whatever you call it, dreaming when you're awake at 4am. What's going on in your head? Nothing to do with medical procedures anyway.

Lisa stared hard, trying to get into Doctor O'Loughlin's mind.

Oh good Jesus, what's wrong with these people. The mother looks like she's going to faint. I can't deal with this, not at this hour. Blah, blah, blah. What is she on? Will she ever calm down? I can't understand what she's saying? Something about a fit. Oh! The young girl had a fit. I get it. Does she mean like a tantrum or one of those mad shaking fits? That must be it. She looks a little old for temper tantrums. God, it's far too late for this. At least I'm paid well. I wonder what time Doctor Fitzmaurice is coming in? I need a few hours sleep before the big game tomorrow. If admin ever find out that's why I'm taking the night o!... Oh damn! She's stopped talking. Now what? Did I deal with this before? I can't remember. I'll refer her. But refer her to where? Oh shit, I need something quick. It's not that serious is it? I think there's something about not running tests until the second seizure.

"Anyone can have one fit in their lifetime. It's if there's a second or third that you need to start worrying. I'm afraid that we can't run tests unless there are more threats."

Don't argue, please don't argue, Doctor O'Loughlin said to himself, hoping that he sounded convincing.

"That can't be right," Lisa's father argued. "We can't just sit and wait. We can't deal with this sort of thing."

I don't think Doctor O'Lockjaw's grin face can deal with it either, Lisa said to herself, frowning at the doctor. He's such an amateur. He hasn't the foggiest what to do. I can tell he's bluffing. He's totally winging it.

"I assure you," Doctor O'Loughlin glanced hurriedly at the file on his desk, "Mr. Tumulty, this is standard procedure and perfectly normal. If it happens again you will be referred for tests straight away. I know it's tough but it's all we can do."

Yeah-right, Lisa thought, rolling her eyes.

She was annoyed. She didn't want to wait and see if the fit might happen again. She wanted the problem to be fixed so that she could forget about it and get on with things. And Doctor Falseface was giving her the crazy option – lets-wait-and-see if she flakes out again.

Lisa scowled, knowing she would have to try and get through each day with the worry of what might happen.

"Exciting times ahead," she said to herself sarcastically as her parents thanked the doctor for his time.

Three weeks passed and nothing happened. Lisa was beginning to think that the amateur doctor was right although she hated to admit it. Perhaps it had been a once off Besides, if she was going to have another fit it would have happened by now, right?

She still thought about it at night. During the day she had other matters to deal with, bullying matters to be precise. Ever since she beat Kelly Matthews to the main part in the school play this year, her school days had become hell. She wouldn't normally be a target for bullying as she was well able to argue back, but this was somehow different. Kelly didn't get put off when Lisa fought back. It seemed to just encourage her, and now the name-calling and dirty looks were getting increasingly worse. There was even a bit of pushing and shoving involved. For someone who claimed to have such a hectic life being beautiful and popular, Kelly certainly had a lot of time on her hands to make Lisa's life miserable.

When Lisa had first gotten the part, Kelly told people that Lisa was a spiteful bitch purposefully ruining Kelly's dream. Lisa knew Kelly was lying. It wasn't that big a deal. The play hadn't even been a success with electricity cutting out during the second half. Still, Lisa wouldn't have auditioned for the part had she known it was going to cause such problems. At least it kept her mind off the whole seizure thing. In a weird way she was grateful to Kelly for that.

Lisa hadn't mentioned anything about the fit to her friends. It wasn't exactly a great conversation starter.

'Hey guess what? I lost it last night and started beating myself against my bed, so how are ye?'

No, it wouldn't have worked. Then one Monday morning at lunchtime Lisa wished she had at least told her teachers about the seizure.

Lisa and her best friend Ali were walking back from the canteen. They were approaching a group of lads among which was James, her flavour of the past year.

Oh my God, he's gorgeous. Look at his hair. He's actually looking at me. Right this is it, Lisa, prepare to flash your best smile. God, I hope I don't have toffee stuck between my teeth. Right, walk tall... oh Jesus my feet, I'm going to faint.

"Ali, I need to sit down," Lisa mumbled, bending her knees to sit.

"What are you at?" Ali gaped confused. "I know you want to catch his attention but in fairness..."

Ali began to pull her up. Lisa's legs went from under her. She didn't sit down as hoped but collapsed into a heap on the ground.

Oh please no, not here, not in front of James. Not in front of the whole school. "Oh my God, Lisa's having a seizure," Ali yelled. "Quick, lads, get someone. Give me that coat. She's going to crack her skull. Hurry!"

Lisa's body jerked, hitting the ground hard, but she couldn't feel anything. She was numb. Despite the awful shaking she could still think.

Why is this happening? she asked herself. It was only supposed to happen at night, not in front of the whole school during lunchtime.

She could vaguely see a number of figures running about – others standing over her looking pale and anxious.

Stop looking at me. Please go away.

One of the crowd looked slightly different to the rest – white hair and glasses. One of the elderly teachers, Lisa presumed. She tried to ask her for help but forget about the little men pulling the switches inside her so that she could just make unusual grunts.

After a few minutes it all came to an end.

Lisa curled into a ball and shielded herself from the faces of her comrades. She wished that she could somehow stay like that and teleport out of the country.   What will people think of me? My life is over. The talk of the day will be of Lisa Tumulty, the one who went insane. She shuddered. Whatever reputation she had had was gone completely.

Her thoughts were interrupted by a voice she recognised.

"Lisa, love, are you alright?" asked Miss Daly.

Oh yeah, never been better, Lisa thought.

"Do you want to try and get up?" Miss Daly said softly.

Lisa shook her head.

"I won't be able."

"Alright, we'll leave you a few minutes."

The bell rang to signal the end of break.

"The rest of you, off to class, come on now."

Everybody began to shuffle about and make a move, still talking about Lisa.

Lisa sighed. It wasn't exactly the kind of attention she liked. She would have preferred it if they discussed how nice her hair was or what a great sense of fashion she had. After a few minutes, Ms. Daly asked again if she wanted to get up. Lisa nodded. Her legs would surely be back by now. The teacher helped to pull her up.

"We'll go to the staff room, ok?"

Whatever, Lisa thought. What did it matter where she went? She was still going to be seen. She walked swiftly towards the entry doors of the main building. Her head was killing her. She looked at the chewing gum covered tarmac.

What a place to have a fit, she thought. She made it to the staff room without anybody seeing her.

Great, now I just have to get through the next three years.

Andrew Murray

MISSION'S END

*Kilbeggan Writing Group
17 years old*

Helena Hayes

UNDER THE STAIRCASE

Kilbeggan Writing Group
15 years old
Short Story

Her cold blue eyes said something to Julie that day, something that words could never say. It was as if her eyes were calling Julie's name, calling out for help but Julie could never save her.

Why do I feel like I have to help her? Julie wondered as she rolled the newspaper up and put it inside her jacket pocket. She leaned back against the lamppost. The cold air wrapped itself tightly around her. Julie didn't care. The air was cold and invigorating, filled with the overpowering smell of freshly cut grass and tinged with the faint smell of alcohol. The sun was beginning to rise but she could still see the moon in the distance. Just then the wind attacked her from the east, bringing with it golden brown leaves, a cigarette butt and a crisp bag, and for the few minutes that followed, the dancing leaves, cigarette butt and crisp bag amused her.

Across the street the milkman emerged from his house looking as though he wished he had chosen a different profession, one which didn't require him waking up at five in the morning. He was the second person she had seen in about three hours, the first of course being Bridie Brown, the old woman notorious for bringing her shovel on early morning walks.

Julie's phone did a jig on the pavement beside her. Another message from her sister Emily. Julie glanced at the digital letters screaming at her on the little yellow screen.

GET HOME NOW!!!!!!!

Why is she telling me what to do? I hate her. I hate her. I hate her.

Julie shoved her phone back into her pocket and stumbled onto her feet. She tried to jump the wall in front of her but she hit her shin and landed on the other side with a thud.

"Shit!"

Julie jumped back onto her feet.

Thank God no one saw that.

The pain shot up her leg as she began to walk. She glanced over at the gate. A white sign with red letters said,

Trespassers will be prosecuted.

I'm sure the 'I'm looking for my dog excuse' won't work at five in the morning, she thought, starting to half-run, half-limp over the field. It did cross her mind to actually go home. But then that would be giving her sister what she wanted.

No. I won't go home. But where will I go?

Twigs snapped under her feet as Julie crept in through the window.

Why am I trying to be so quiet? she asked herself. This place is virtually deserted.

The only inhabitants of the old house were the bats that lived in the roof shafts, millions of insects and, she had her suspicions, a few mice. Glass shattered and floorboards creaked under her feet as Julie walked in through the old kitchen. Beams of dim light seeped in through the soiled window in front of her. She went through the little door into the sitting room. A tree grew up the centre of the room and emerged out through the roof.

Beyond the sitting room in the hallway there was a stairs. It was obvious from looking at it that it had once been a beautiful staircase, and that a beautiful lady in a long gown had once elegantly sauntered down to meet the man of her dreams. Their eyes had locked in love at first sight and they lived happily ever after. But now the stairs, once a bridge of love, was just a wreckage of rotting timber and vegetation. Julie peered up the steps.

I have to go up.

She stepped onto the first step. It creaked violently. She took another step. It crumbled. She jumped onto the next step, her brain telling her not to go any further, her legs climbing upwards. Her heart thumped inside her chest. And then suddenly her foot fell through the timber. Her body went cold. She tried to grab the banister railing. It broke off She fell deeper into the hole. She screamed for help. No one came.

With her troubled screams she fell. She fell deep into the darkness.

"Oh my God! Where is she?"

Emily frantically strode up and down the living room. Peering out the window she noticed a figure in the distance.

It's her.

She ran out into the hallway and flung open the door. The freezing air attacked the open wound on her forehead as she ran out into the driveway. The figure came closer.

"Julie, Julie," Emily called out. "It's you. You've come back."

What's that she's carrying? Emily wondered. Suddenly she came to a halt in the middle of the driveway.

No, it can't be. It's not her.

Emily stood dismayed.

"I'm sorry," she whispered. "I'm sorry".

A single tear gently trickled down her face.

Stop it! she told herself as she brushed the tear from her cheek.

Bridie Brown briskly strode down the footpath; her shovel was thrown across her right shoulder. Emily got up and headed back inside. She glanced at her watch; her parents were due back in less than an hour.

What am I supposed to do? she asked herself.

The previous night was such a blur. It was so unreal, like a horror movie. Emily flicked on the television in an attempt to break the eerie silence that'd filled the house ever since Julie had stormed out a few hours earlier. The silence wrapped itself around her and made her feel cold and unsure.

Click.

The early morning news.

"Aine McDonald, a twenty-five year old woman from Redhills, Seapoint, is still missing," the news broadcaster said in a rigid, monotone voice. "Further Garda investigations have shown that she was not abducted."

The picture of a woman with blonde hair and intense blue eyes appeared on the screen. The missing woman's eyes seemed to jump out of the television. Her face was dotted with freckles.

I wonder if I could send out a missing persons report for Julie? Emily pondered as she walked into the kitchen. No, I can't. They can't find out what's happened.

The body was still there, lying on the floor. Somehow, Emily had expected it to be gone. But it wasn't. He still lay there motionless. His skin a pale, grey colour. The dog sniffed his dark hair, it was saturated in gel. The cat prowled around him and began licking his earring.

Julie shut her eyes, tightly.

"Ahhh!" she screamed as she landed in the midst of the rubble.

A piece of glass pierced her skin, cutting into the back of her leg. Her head pressed forward. Her body tightened. She shivered.

"Crap," she shouted loudly.

She heard shuffling.

A rat, she winced.

Julie crawled over to a corner, curling tightly in a ball. She held her knees firmly against her chest. The back of her leg ached. A stream of blood trickled down her calf. Her heart thumped inside her chest. She pulled her phone from her pocket. She flicked it open. The room lit up.

She froze.

Across the room a woman was crouched in the corner, still and afraid. The woman screamed. Julie screamed. She could feel her heart thumping against her chest. Julie took a sharp deep breath.

It's her, that woman, Julie thought, recalling the cold blue eyes, the limp blonde hair and freckled face. Suddenly they could hear footsteps outside the little room. The woman pressed her bony finger against her lips. Her eyes widened. Her breathing became heavy and slow. The footsteps began to disappear. They both sat in silence, too terrified to move. A door slammed in the distance.

"It's ok," the woman whispered moments later. "He's gone."

"Who's gone?" Julie asked, her voice trembling.

She felt like crying.

"I don't know, he comes in every day," the woman replied.

"I think he owns the place..." her voice trailed off

"You're that lost woman, aren't you?" Julie said.

"No. I'm not lost. I know where I am," the woman retorted.

"But the papers, the photo..."

Julie reached inside her coat and pulled out the rolled up newspaper. She tossed it over to the woman who was still talking about the man who comes in every day. She seemed happy to have some sort of human company. She looked at the newspaper, her jaw tightening, her face slowly colouring.

"The family of Aine Mc Donald desperately search. Hah! They

couldn't care less if I never came back!" she snarled.

Julie stared blankly.

Maybe I shouldn't have shown her the paper.

"They never wanted me," Aine said; her voice was trembling, tears welling up in the corners of her eyes.

Julie took a long deep breath and exhaled slowly, burying her head in her hands.

How could her actions have led to something like this? Running away from home! What was she thinking? At least I have something real to escape from, thought Julie.

She could picture him still lying there. The image made her shudder. She kept trying to replay it in her mind but she just couldn't. All she could remember was watching her boyfriend sadly struggle against his inescapable destiny, attempting to grasp the last shreds of life left in his body.

What have I done? Julie asked herself over and over. What have I done?

She looked across at Aine sitting quietly holding the crumpled newspaper in her hands. They were both lost deep in the darkness of their own thoughts, wondering how they had arrived at a point in their lives where they could never return or move on.

"Why are you here?" asked Aine, lifting her head and narrowing her eyes.

I can't tell her, Julie panicked. I can't tell anyone about Alex's dead body sprawled across the kitchen floor. I can't tell her.

"Emm... I just have to... emm... get away," Julie said, trying to sound a convincing. Aine nodded in acceptance and then clumsily got onto her feet.

"Well, are you coming then or not?" Aine asked.

"Coming where?"

"I'm going in that direction," Aine said, pointing out towards the clearing in the trees that encompassed the old house.

"The sun always seems to be over there."

Am I really going to go with a clearly insane woman that follows the sun? I can't. I can't leave Emily. And what about Alex? I can't stay here. Who knows what else I'm capable of doing?

She watched Aine pick her way across the rubble.

A new beginning, Julie thought. A fresh start, it's so tempting.

"Are you coming?" asked Aine, getting a little impatient.

"One second," said Julie turning around.

She pulled out her phone and began texting her sister.

Emily, I'm going away. Don't worry. I will see you again. Love you.
xxxxx.

Julie placed the phone down on the rough ground and staggered onto her feet.

"What's your name?" asked Aine.

"I'm Julie."

Julie painted a smile onto her face but inside she felt hollow. It was this emptiness that stood between her and complete freedom. The countryside stretched out in front of them for miles, too many miles to ponder. She looked out towards the horizon, the most distant point where the ground seemed to climb into the blackened sky. The rain began to pour, it just come down and down and down.

Jill Griffin

PESTERPOWER

Tullamore Writing Group
17 years old
Excerpt from her novel
Pesterpower

Hannah positively buzzed with excitement. Her first outdoor concert had brought wonderful summer weather and her favourite band would be playing after the support acts. The concert wasn't simply bands playing on a stage. It was an experience. Held in a park, in an area of green, fenced off and filled with food and drink kiosks, t-shirt stalls, toilets and a medical corner. The inside had been brought outside. Hannah noticed the grass had been cut so severely it didn't even look like grass anymore. It was yellow and decaying.

Hannah tried to find her place among the thousands of fans as music pounded out of the huge black speakers and echoed through the crowd – the kind of music that can usually be heard in supermarkets and hair salons. She wondered if the speakers were hiding something; they were too thick and too big for the sole purpose of transporting sound. Two huge monitors either side of the stage had bright colours splashed across their screens; advertising various things that could be bought at the concert. The distorted images were beginning to make her feel nauseous. Hannah wondered if this was the desired effect.

"Let's go get a drink, I'm roasting!" her friend Cathy exclaimed, lifting Hannah out of her paranoid notions of conspiracy.

The blazing sun glared down on the tops of their heads, forcing Hannah to regret the argument with her mother about bringing a sunhat 'just in case.' Although, her mam had been advising her to take an umbrella as well, so mothers aren't always right. Absent-mindedly,

Hannah gingerly placed the three fingers of her right hand on top of her head. She revelled in the novelty of how warm her strands of blonde hair felt.

At the drinks stand, both sixteen-year-olds paused to take deep breaths. Hannah fixed her gaze on the sign standing beside the surly security guards. It stated what the burly men, who were only too true to their strong, silent persona, could not say themselves.

It is illegal to purchase alcohol if you are under 18.

Hannah grinned, muttering her new date of birth to herself. Suddenly, Cathy lost her nerve and thrust her tattered five euro note into Hannah's palm.

"I need the toilet," she explained pathetically.

Acting calm and inconspicuous is not for the faint-hearted. Striding up to the end of the queue, Hannah glanced all around her, pretending to be nonchalant. But the two guards noticed her straight away; it was their job after all. She was amazed by their hideousness.

"Whatcha want?" one barked gruffly, his little ginger nose hairs moving about alarmingly.

"A drink," Hannah replied, trying to look confused.

"What's your date of birth?" the other asked, smirking.

"The fifteenth of April 1988," she rhymed off triumphantly.

"Alright," they conceded, rather prematurely she thought. "But just one drink!"

A few hours later, Hannah was picking her way back through the crowd for the fourth time during the concert, attempting not to spill any of the bubbly concoction she was carrying. Nothing about beer's sweaty taste or its gassy side-effects was particularly attractive to Hannah, but it was the only refreshment available since the company who produced it was sponsoring the concert.

Doesn't advertising have a profound influence on our lives?

She recalled the speech she'd written for the debating team at school as she handed Cathy another beer.

Finally, her favourite band bounded on to the stage, the lead singer shouting "Afternoon!" casually into the microphone in a deep Sheffield twang. Hannah and her friends jumped up and down, screamed, squealed and fell over. An unfamiliar energy surged through the crowd. The drums sounded the beat of Hannah's racing heart. She squealed again. Moments like this could never be communicated through the medium of the English language. French might work though.

A couple of songs later and everyone had relaxed slightly, easing themselves into the electric swing of things. Somehow they all knew there was something bigger and better to come. The crowd breathed in anticipation. Effervescent colours danced across the stage over the band and their instruments. The camera zoomed in on the lead singer's shiny black guitar; every eye was on the monitors. Hannah, who had been crouched on the ground searching for her last two-euro coin, stood up to find a peculiar scene.

The intake of alcohol may result in seeing double, Hannah recalled reading somewhere, surely that didn't mean seeing two versions of the same moment?

Her long eyelashes swooped down over her green eyes. As she had first thought, the crowd was still leaping about, screaming and enjoying themselves. At the front, some were throwing the remaining dregs of beer at each other, plastic glasses and all. But Hannah saw a very different picture at the same time.

Flickering, like a broken light switch, she saw everyone standing perfectly still staring at the monitors, hypnotized. She herself gaped at the enormous screen; the guitar became blurry and faded away. Now the screens were blank until letters appeared.

KLIL.SATB.KLIL

The bold red letters flashed across the monitor for a second but Hannah froze in astonishment. The world around her had returned to normal yet the memory of sheer surprise lingered in her mind. For that moment the lyrics the singer had been snarling hadn't sounded right, it was one of her favourite songs and she was certain the words hadn't fitted. But she couldn't remember. A weeping girl stormed past interrupting Hannah's contemplation. She returned her attention to the show.

Hannah trudged away from the stage disappointed. It would be a long time before she could afford to see her favourite band again and in such pleasant conditions. In fact, it had been one of those rare unique days that could almost never be repeated. When would the same crowd of fifteen thousand people ever be gathered in the same place again? Never. However, Hannah found her disappointment fading as the drunks behind her bellowed their own encore to the show. They howled the rather cheerful lyrics, making them sound wholly melancholic. She was a little taken aback when a female security guard asked to check her handbag on the way out. But she opened it anyway since she had nothing to hide. Instead of just shooting a glance at the contents, the plump young woman slid her hand inside, dropping something heavy to the bottom of it.

"What the fuck are you...?" Hannah began, but she was given a forceful shove and moved along.

She looked around her, something odd was happening. Hundreds of security guards in luminous yellow waistcoats approached groups of people and reached inside their jackets and bags. Soberly, she began to feel terrified, struggling to keep up with her friends who had also been stopped by some guards. Hannah carefully put her hand inside her bag. Her fingertips caressed something hard and plastic.

"Come on Hannah, we'll miss the fucking bus!" Cathy screamed at her, looking dishevelled.

Hannah ran up to Cathy, navigating her way through groups of rowdy drunks.

"Did a security guard stop any of you?" Hannah gasped breathlessly.

"Eh yeah, it was a bit weird alright. He put something in my bag and said I might want it later, but he *still* wouldn't give me my naggin of vodka back!" Cathy replied darkly, clearly more upset about her confiscated alcohol than the strange behaviour.

Hannah rolled her eyes. Her friends were still too drowsy to shed any light on this bewildering behaviour. She fumbled in her bag remembering the female security guard's eerie stare. She trembled as her fingertips found something cold and metallic. Hannah's freckled arm emerged from her white handbag to reveal a long, sharp, menacing knife. It looked more like the choice weapon of a crazed serial killer than your average butter knife. Hannah let out a faint yelp, holding the knife at arm's length. The others turned around.

"What the..." began Kevin, a tall greasy-haired boy. "Oi! Where'd you get that?"

"Oh God, she's going to do us all in!" a stout spotty boy named Barry exclaimed in terror.

"This is what your one gave me!" Hannah shrieked, jerking her head in the direction of the clump of security guards behind her.

"Well, throw it away then! Stop pointing it at us!" Cathy retorted heatedly.

"You said a security guard gave you something too!"

Cathy found an identical knife in her own frayed handbag and Kevin also discovered a slightly bigger blade stowed in the pocket of his jacket. Both of them swore that they had never seen the weapons before. Barry, who had been gawking at them all with his mouth hanging open, quickly began to scowl when he realised that he was the only one who had not received a knife. Hannah was sure he was going to moan sulkily about being left out, he was clearly oblivious to the danger they were in.

A swarm of questions and conspiracy theories swirled through Hannah's mind. Nearby, she could see a young bearded man gazing into his backpack with a bemused look on his face. Panic rattled her chest painfully. She could sense the onset of something bad and potentially fatal happening.

Everyone around her appeared dazed. Even her own friends, who were always so vocal and forceful with their opinions, remained silent, staring at the ground, dumbfounded.

"I think we should just get out of here," Hannah announced finally. "Anyone seen the others?"

The three of them looked up at her blankly. Their eyes had the same glazed look as the freaky female security guard. Suddenly, Hannah felt the knife she was still holding being snatched from her hand. Barry lunged at her. Hannah winced as her back collided with a hard stone wall. The shock had made her lose sense of her surroundings. Barry was unbearably close to her, his repulsive breath reeking of mustard and beer. His chubby fingers spread around her neck.

"Get off me you fat bastard!" she screeched.

But he acted as if he hadn't heard her. He just continued to breathe heavily on her. He raised the knife so she could see the blade glinting in the glow of the street lamps. Something about Hannah's urgent bellowing seemed to wake Cathy up. Her brown eyes returned to normal. She pounced on Barry, trying to pull him back. Her long purple fingernails dug into the hand that was holding the knife. But Barry, who had always been so timid and girlish, was not easily restrained. He tried to shrug her off but Cathy was determined to stop him. Then he loosened his firm grip on Hannah's neck. He turned around, seizing Cathy's arm and in one swift movement, drove the knife into her stomach. Then he simply let her fall to the ground, discarding her like a swatted fly. All Hannah could hear was herself screaming as she gaped at the crimson blood seeping through Cathy's pink top. A numbing cold sensation moved from her temples to her ears. The outline of Barry's corpulent figure flickered just at the edge of her eye line as he moved to take the bloodied knife from Cathy's stomach. Springing into action, Hannah grabbed the sleeve of Barry's baggy T-shirt and yanked him toward her, so that they faced each other. With every ounce of strength that she could gather, she sunk her head into Barry's greasy face, hoping that a broken nose would be enough of a distraction so that she could make her escape. Leaning back, she stamped on his foot for good measure and shoved him near where Cathy was lying. Hannah ran as fast as she could in the opposite direction, wondering if Cathy was still alive.

The chaos spread fast. Everywhere Hannah looked, people were screaming and scrambling feebly at each other. The rows and rows of white buses, which had been previously waiting impatiently for their passengers, had all infuriatingly disappeared. Hannah's eyes scanned the dark, tree-covered expanse for her missing friends. But having considered what had happened to Cathy, she wasn't sure if they were her friends anymore. It wasn't Barry who had attacked her, who had stabbed Cathy so brutally. He had been brainwashed somehow and Hannah knew it was something to do with the fact that knives were being passed around by security guards. She wanted to escape. All thoughts of Cathy left her head as soon as her mobile was in her shaking hand. She dialled Mark's number, but there was no answer. She tried another friend, and another friend, all of them failed to answer. Desperately, Hannah called 999. She pressed the phone to her ear so tightly it hurt, the harsh ringing noise buzzed through her head.

"Hello, emergency services?"

Hannah's heart lifted, finally some help with this nightmare.

"Hi, I'm at this concert in..."

Her one remaining lifeline was seized from her grasp, taking her arm with it. Whirling round she faced a tanned blonde boy, only a little older than herself who was wearing a pink T-shirt that was at least two sizes to small for him. His eyes were unfocused like all the others and there was a knife at his side. He bared his teeth at her. A piercing scream grazed Hannah's throat. She wasn't even wailing in fear anymore, but in frustration. The blonde attacker paused at Hannah's hysterical screams; everyone else he had attacked with his knife had been too shocked to scream.

"Hey! Get away from her ya pansy prick!" a voice familiar to Hannah bellowed gruffly.

Mark ran at her attacker and the murderous blonde fled with Hannah's phone and his weapon.

Hannah fell into her best friend's arms, resting her head on his warm shoulder.

"It's okay. It's okay," he whispered soothingly, "C'mon we have to get out of here."

Pulling her by the arm, Mark led her to the gateway that their bus had driven through only a couple of hours before. Why did it seem so long ago now? Her mind raced with the effort of trying to process all of this information. She thought her head would explode, it felt so full. She finally spoke.

"Did they give you a knife on the way out?" she asked.

"A knife? What are you on about?" Mark sneered, giving her the bemused look he always gave her when she was drunk.

Usually when she was drunk, she declared her love for him. Hannah took a deep breath.

"Security guards stopped me, Cathy, and Kevin on the way out and they gave us knives without us knowing and then, then..."

Mark nodded condescendingly and began to walk faster.

"Hurry up. We're going to have to walk for a bit 'cause we've missed the bus."

Hannah tried to suppress her fury.

"Mark, listen to me. It's Cathy. Barry took my knife and he stabbed her and he tried to stab me and I had to leave her lying there. I...I think she's dead..." Hannah sobbed.

Mark halted and looked at her closely, clearly aghast.

"Are you sure?" he asked.

Hannah nodded, wiping the tears from her eyes.

"We have to go back for her!" she cried exasperatedly.

"Do you know where she is?"

Hannah stopped and looked around, not recognising anything. Everywhere looked the same.

"No," she answered truthfully.

"Well, we'll ring the Guards as soon as we find a phone, ok? Don't worry, she'll be alright."

They walked silently for a while. Hannah knew Mark didn't really believe her. He never took her seriously. She glanced at his expression but as usual it didn't tell her anything.

"That guy who took my phone," she continued, "he was acting the same way as Barry."

Mark sighed.

"Well, he didn't stab anyone did he?"

"But he had a knife."

"Hannah, he was just trying to mug you, alright?"

"Didn't you see him? He's a D4 boy from head to toe. He's more well off than I am!" she yelled defiantly.

"So, him and Barry are trying to kill you and Cathy and those security guards are helping them, even though neither of them could beat shite?" Mark argued sarcastically.

"No it's not like that, they've been possessed or something..."

"Look, I don't know what you've been drinking but give it a rest, alright? We're stuck in the middle of nowhere with no way home!" he shouted.

Hannah was just about to scream back when she saw the phone box. Mark ran inside and she watched him through the glass. She searched in her own pocket for money to ring her parents, knowing that there would be about fifty missed calls on her stolen phone from home by now. Then she remembered searching for that last two-euro coin and the message on the monitor.

In the dusty taxi, after another argument involving the words, 'guards' and 'knife,' Hannah sat close to the door trying to pretend Mark wasn't there. He had told her that she was acting like a child so she decided to prove him wrong by sulking and refusing to speak to him. Thankfully, Mark knew the driver so it would be okay for them to pay for the taxi the following day. Hannah was doing her best not to cry but she couldn't get rid of the sensation of helplessness. If Mark didn't believe her, no one else would. And she was dying to tell him about the monitor as well.

After what seemed like hours, the taxi stopped just across the street from the housing estate where Hannah and Mark lived. Mark said goodbye to the driver cheerfully and leapt out of the car. Hannah mumbled a thank you and slowly climbed out. Looking at her watch, she saw that it was two o'clock in the morning. Not wanting to fight with him any longer, she reluctantly jogged after Mark who was already walking hastily along the other side of the street.

"Mark! Hold on!" she called after him.

Her footsteps echoed in the quiet. There was no one around. Mark halted but failed to turn around and deride her for being so slow, something he would have usually done. When she reached his hunched figure, she stopped to catch her breath, breathing in the scent of aftershave and cigarette smoke, which always seemed to linger in the air around him. She felt the same cold confusion wash over her when he still didn't turn to face her. Their argument hadn't been that serious.

"Mark?" she murmured tapping him on the shoulder, "Look I'm sorry, I know it sounds crazy..."

Hannah felt a warm tingling sensation as he touched her hand. He grabbed it violently, twisting it as he finally turned to face her. His expression was blank and the pupils of his eyes were so big they almost filled their brilliant green colour.

"Ow! Mark you're hurting me!" she whimpered shrilly.

But he wrestled her to the ground, covering her mouth with his hand. She tried to scream but he was too strong. He reached inside his jacket and took out a knife identical to the one in Cathy's stomach. She blinked at him, willing herself not to cry. She struggled fiercely under his weight but he didn't even budge, he just sat glaring down at her, pointing the knife directly over her forehead. She continued to writhe helplessly underneath his weight, trying to scream even though the stench of his sweaty hand was repulsive. She gazed into his eyes seeking some sort of reaction but it was as if he was looking straight through her. His eyes were lifeless, like he was hypnotized. He dangled the knife over her chest. Hannah was exhausted from struggling and could only squeal inaudibly, hot tears rolling off her face.

Mark raised the knife high above his head. She let out one last terrified muffled shriek. His knees clenched around her waist. As the shining blade descended, Hannah instinctively turned over on her side with all her might. Toppling over on the grass, Mark grunted angrily but Hannah was already running as fast as she could towards the nearest house. Thundering footsteps pounded not far behind. She jumped over the low brick wall into the back garden and ferociously banged on the door. She stumbled into her elderly neighbours' arms wailing.

"He's trying to kill me. He's going to kill me!"

Mark kicked the door just as it shut. The sudden feeling of relief disappeared as quickly as it had come. Hannah was certain he would get in. He knocked on the windows wielding his weapon threateningly.

"KILL. STAB. KILL," he muttered.

Chris Nolan

WHAT I'D GIVE FOR A SECOND CHANCE

Tullamore Writing Group
14 years old
Excerpts from his novel
What I'd Give for a Second
Chance

– Chapter One –

That day started out normally. The dull February weather darkened what was to be a joyous day for me, my birthday. Every year my mom calls me to tell me what a waste my life has been. Bitter bitch. She changed after my dad died in 'Nam. I can't say I didn't deserve these accusations. I took no risks, put no effort into life. Look at me now. I'm a forty-three, well now it's a forty-four year old, single virgin employee at marvel comics.

I'm their janitor.

I left my cluttered New York apartment for a coffee and a bagel.

"Hey taxi!" I yelled, raising my hand.

I hopped in as one pulled up beside me.

"Where to?" the taxi driver asked.

"Fifth Avenue," I replied.

The taxi picked up speed.

"Slow down!" I screeched.

"She won't!" the driver said with concern.

Then with a jolt we stopped. A woman outside screamed. I looked down to investigate the strange sensation in my stomach. The metal taxi frame stabbed my insides. Blood spurted out. I felt dizzy. I could feel myself slipping away.

No, it couldn't end this way, not now...

...What I'd give for a second chance... going... going... gone.

– Chapter Two: The Swingin' Sixties (1963) –

I woke up in a hospital. There was something wrong. The people were massive. Super-sized. They looked weird.

"What's goin' on?" I yelled.

There was a sound of innocent gurgling. Suddenly I became wide awake. I raised up my left hand. It was there but it was tiny. I'd lost my left hand in an engineering class accident when I was eighteen. How come I had my left hand back? Something weird was going on.

"Right through here, Mrs. Davidson," a nurse called.

Mom walked in. She was much younger. She picked me up and smiled sweetly at me.

"Hi, Bob," she whispered.

I screamed. The scream translated into a loud wail.

I was a kid! A child. A baby.

This can't be, I thought. I expected to wake up at any time but then it all went black.

I woke up in a house, my house. Other women gathered around my mom.

"He's got such big brown eyes!" one said.

"Aww! The little angel!" squealed another.

I dozed off again with the sound of mindless chatter ringing in my ears.

Why is this happening to me? The only way to stop that car crash suddenly became clear to me. I had to fix up my life.

That night I dreamt of the car crash. Every night in my dreams I died. I suppose that was a constant reminder of the task ahead. The first few months of my new life passed by quickly. I only woke up to be fed and to be changed.

– Chapter Three – Birthday Surprises (1965) –

"Happy birthday, Bob!" my mom said, lifting me out of my bed.

Wow, my second birthday, here already.

"We have to get you washed and dressed for your party," mom continued.

There was a knocking at the front door.

"Betty?" a man's voice called.

"John!" mom squealed excitedly.

"Up here!"

"Coming!"

John ran up the stairs.

"There he is! My son, the birthday boy!" said John.

"Bob, this is your daddy," mom introduced.

"Ga... ga," I said.

That was all I could muster for my first meeting with my father. He was home on leave from the war, and before this day he'd never seen me in the flesh.

"I gotcha something," dad said, producing a toy truck.

I laughed happily and ran off to play with my new toy.

"Hey! Where are you going?" mom yelled.

"You still have to get ready!"

Mom prepared a bath for me. I brought the truck in with me. I was scrubbed extra well.

"John, could you pass out his clothes on the bed?" mom asked.

"Yeah, sure honey."

Dad came in with my clothes. I was dried and clothed. I followed mom downstairs to find a cake with two candles on top.

"Go on, sweetie," mom said.

I blew out the candles. My parents cheered. I was cut a slice of the cake. The cream tasted so fresh and the strawberry jam tasted beautiful. I went off to play with my truck. I imitated the sound of a car. Then I remembered the accident. I screamed. My parents came racing in.

"What's wrong, honey?" mom asked, scouring my eyes for a clue.

"Champ?" dad tried.

"He's probably tired," mom said.

"I'm putting him off to bed."

No, not there, I thought.

I didn't sleep that night for fear of being killed again. The following day dad left for 'Nam. I'll never forget him walking out the door in uniform. He turned around and looked at me one last time.

"Seeya, champ," he said.

I never saw him again.

– Chapter Four – Death of a Patriot (1967 –)

"I'm so sorry, Mrs. Davidson."

I walked down the stairs, interrupting a man and mom talking.

"Bob..." mom started. "Your daddy... he... he died last week in Vietnam."

I said nothing and walked off. I had expected this. It hurt more now that it had come to pass. It was the one aspect of my life I couldn't change. I felt so helpless.

Mom came upstairs.

"Oh Bob... I'm so sorry, honey. I'm so sorry."

She sagged on my bed and cried her soul out. A few days later dad's body was brought home. He was given a patriot's burial. My relatives looked on as the January rain pounded the American flag being handed to my mom. After the service I ran upstairs and cried in a corner. I whacked the cold wooden floor.

"It's not fair!' I screamed.

The following days were tough. I was confined to the house by the rain and an overprotective mother. Mom took dad's death hard. I came downstairs to find mom lying on the couch drinking cheap whiskey. Mom was a big influence in my life so it became clear that to fix up my life I had to help fix hers. I had to remind her that she had a son that needed raising, a son that needed a commanding figure to look up to.

"Mommy? I miss daddy," I said sadly.

"Aw, sweetie, me too, but he's gone and we gotta put that behind us. You're going to school in September and you'll make lots of new friends and everything will be ok," mom said.

"Things are going to be better, I promise."

– Chapter Five – School (September 1967) –

"Bob! Wake up! It's your first day of school!" mom hollered.

I bounced up out of bed. This was where a big change was to happen. I kept my memories and knowledge from my previous life, and those memories could be used to my advantage. I could be skipped ahead or I might even get a college scholarship! I went downstairs and ate a bowl of porridge. I went back upstairs and changed into my uniform. I was to attend St. Columba's School. It was a very nice place. The teachers were pleasant. The students were very nice except for this one bully who was in my year.

Martin Henderson.

He was tall as a mountain but his head was as thick as one too. He could make a fifth grader piss his pants and surrender his lunch money with a murderous glance.

"Bob, come into the bathroom sweetie," mom called.

I ran in.

Mom was there with a comb in her hand. She grabbed me.

'No!' I screamed.

The comb of doom brushed through my light, brown hair. I shrieked. Then she wiped the side of my face.

"Oh mom..." I whined.

I went downstairs. I picked up my lunchbox and mom walked me to school.

The school was about half a mile away. She dropped me off at the front gates.

"Oh, my little baby is all grown up now."

"Stop mom, your embarrassing me."

She kissed my forehead and walked home. I went off to meet my new classmates.

"Hey, what's your name?" a voice behind me asked.

"Oh," I said as I turned around.

It was a boy with a freckled face and short black hair. That face was unmistakable! It was Chester Burrows!

"Hi, I'm Bob Davidson," I said.

"Hey, Bob, I'm Chester Burrows," Chester said.

"D'ya wanna play tag?" I asked.

"Sure!" Chester replied.

Chester ran at me.

"Tag, you're it!"

I ran at him through the crowds of students. Then the bell chimed. An old man walked out of the school.

"Everyone line up," he ordered.

Me and Chester found the other kindergartens. There were about ten of us, six boys, four girls.

"Kindergartens, follow Miss Brown."

A young woman walked out of the school.

"Kindergartens," she called.

We followed her. The school seemed very big. We were led into room 3B.

"Everyone sit down," Miss Brown said.

"Today we are going to get to know each other. You there, what's your name?"

"I'm Catherine Gardner. My daddy is the publisher for The New York Times. I live in a house. I have 3 dogs and...'

"That's enough Catherine, let's let someone else have a go."

The whole class had a chance to talk. Then came my go.

"I'm Bob Davidson. I'm four. My daddy died in Vietnam last year. I live with my mom and I know how to do lots of stuff."

"Well done, Bob," Miss Brown said. "Now let's do some painting."

After painting the bell chimed. Mom was waiting for me at the gate.

"How was your first day, honey?" she asked.

"Great!" I replied.

I swore to put my education first and get a decent, horrible-death-free life.

Carolina Troy

INSIGHT

Tullamore Writing Group
16 years old
Chapter one of her novel
Insight

"Another day, another battle," I say as I stretch my arms upwards before sighing deeply.

I gradually pull myself up to sitting position, still nestled snugly beneath my warm duvet. I reach over and gently pet Pixie, my cat, on the head, her black fur smooth as silk to the touch. I gently stroke her stomach, and as I do so I hear her begin to purr with contentment.

"You're a lucky sucker, aren't you?" I say as Pixie jumps up and playfully pushes my hand with her head.

"I wish that I could stay under a duvet all day and do nothing! What's the bet that mother-dearest has breakfast laid out and waiting on the table for us? Eh?"

Pixie knows I'm being sarcastic.

"I suppose it'll be the usual, eggs Benedict with wholemeal toast and a glass of freshly squeezed orange juice."

I give a snort of indignation and get out of bed, tip-toeing gingerly across my bedroom, careful not to trample on any of the objects strewn across the floor. I begin to unbutton my pyjama top and take it off. A searing pain shoots up my left arm. I peer down and look at the raw, gaudy scars, criss-crossing and zigzagging all the way up my arm.

"Nice job," I say grimacing.

I take up the ball of clothes lying in the middle of the floor that is my uniform. I pull it on. The great equaliser. The uniform consists of a hideous navy pleated skirt which is checked blue and green, a light blue shirt that has a tendency to strangle you when done up fully, itchy navy socks and a round-neck navy jumper with the school crest emblazoned on it, just in case we happened to forget which hell-hole we attend.

I trudge downstairs to meet my maker. The so-called mother. Pixie follows closely behind brushing against my legs. With each step the smell of alcohol and dampness grows more intense. The hallway and sitting-room are awash with it. I'm used to the stench though, so used to it that it doesn't make me heave anymore.

When I open the door to the sitting-room, another smell hits me. Vomit. It wafts through the air and enters my nostrils, making me queasy. I open the door of the sitting-room only to be greeted by a very familiar sight. My sorry excuse of a mother, lying face-down and sprawled out on the patchy, stained carpet.

"Had a good night then, I see?" I say spitefully as I stand towering over her. "No, no mother, don't get up on my account. You stay there and rest yourself!"

I turn round and walk straight back out the door.

This morning, May was in her comatose state. When she's comatose, she's on default setting number two. Default setting number one is her awake, all guns blazing, looking for money, looking for a fight.

On default setting number one, I'd get the usual, "Ebony, sweetie, could you lend us a few bob for the shopping?"

It's a nauseating performance, her standing there cooing at me in her sickly sweet voice, arm partially extended, waiting for me to perform the god-like act of dropping manna into her paw, in a bid to stop her starvation. Hah! More like dehydration. The only thing she ever wants is money, or something with at least a ten per cent alcohol content level in it.

"Shopping?" I'd reply, snorting with disbelief.

She was genuinely under the deluded impression that I believed such bullshit. Knowing only too well where my money would go, I somehow always managed to decline the offer to feed her destructive habit. But refusing to give money to May was like pouring petrol over a naked flame. The result was explosive. I've seen her face turn puce with fury. Seen her knuckles turn white. Her bloodshot eyes trying to cut me up, trying to make me give in and give her what she wanted. She'd spit and hiss at me. Call me an ungrateful bitch, a burden, a waste of space and moan about my lack of contribution to *our* household.

In a way it's almost amusing to watch her hypnotised by alcohol. In another way it's terrifying watching her trying to stand on her own two feet without her fix. What is more terrifying is the fact that she no longer just wants it, now she needs it. It helps her to function. And when she doesn't get it, she lashes out at me, lurching forward to strike me across the face. I know the scene off by heart. We've performed it a thousand million times.

"Get out of my sight," she'd spit at me furiously.

"I'm gone," I'd say bitterly.

And with that I'd turn and storm out the door, slamming it loudly behind me, tears welling up in my eyes. Not because I'm upset. Oh no. Simply from the early impact her fist to the side of my head.

Another favourite of hers to throw at me is, "You're just like your father."

She thinks that this is the greatest insult in the universe, since she despised both him and me. I was the only thing that held that unholy matrimony together. She'd say it so smugly and lean back into the arm-chair, crossing her legs, a glass clutched in her hand. A Cheshire cat grin would maliciously appear on her face and spread from ear to ear.

"He was a sad, sorry, excuse of a man," she'd say, her words slurring slightly as they toppled from her mouth.

"I gave him everything. I made him something. And look at what I got. You!" she'd say, glaring, pursing her lips with disgust.

"Well, I'd rather be like him than a sad, old, twisted hag like you! Oh and for the record you haven't got me! So don't think you do!" I'd growl back so coldly, shivering at my own harsh words.

You'd think it'd be impossible to hate the person who brought you into this world, but it isn't. In fact, I despise the woman. May might be my mother, according to the birth certificate issued after my arrival into this world, but according to me I have no mother. Dad always took care of me. He's the one who got me ready for school, made my lunch, taught me to tie my shoe laces and when I'd ask, " Why can't mommy do it?" he'd simply reply, "She's sleeping now, darling."

And I was supposed to be contented with that answer, and I was until my world was turned upside down.

I can't help remembering. It was six days after my ninth birthday. I was lying in bed watching the time tick by, worry gnawing away at the pit of my stomach, rain beating relentlessly against the window. The little clown-face clock that my best friend Sarah had bought me for my birthday read quarter to eleven.

Where could daddy be? I asked myself over and over, clutching the teddy bear he had bought for me 'for being such a brave girl' on one of our trips to the dentist

I didn't feel brave at a quarter to eleven six days after my ninth birthday. Daddy was at least two hours late home from work. Mother dearest had not a care in the world. She sat downstairs vegetating on the couch, slugging from a wine glass. I ventured down the stairs to the sitting room and tapped May on the shoulder.

"Mum?" I said quietly.

There was no reply.

" Mum?" I repeated again a little louder.

Still no reply.

"Mum?" I shouted.

"Why aren't you in bed?" she snapped – so fiercely that I was taken aback.

"I... I... I couldn't sleep," I stuttered in a state of shock. "I... I... I was... worried about daddy!" I said quietly trying to avert my gaze by staring down at the floor.

"Hah," she scoffed "Worried? Your father will stroll in here any moment, wait and see."

So I did, I waited, but only for a few moments. A knock came to the door. Three loud raps. With each thud of the hand against the black, weather-beaten, wooden door my heart sank a little lower.

"While you're up you might as well make yourself useful and answer that!" May said, without taking her eyes off the TV.

I remember how the movie she was pretending to watch flickered, illuminating her rosy, gaunt face with a faint glow. I gently twisted the door knob and opened the door only to come face to face with a fully uniformed garda.

"Hello there, little lady," he said softly, his voice deep and concerned. "Is your mother home?" he asked with a note of suspicion entering his voice.

"Yes, she is. I'll just get her for you now."

I scurried back towards the sitting-room.

"Mum," I hissed from the doorway, "there's a guard at the door and he wants to see you!"

She pushed herself off the chair and without saying a word, walked towards the front door stumbling slightly. She stood peering at the tall figure before her. I watched from the dimly lit hall clutching at the door-jam.

"Can I help you, officer?" she said, sweet as pie.

"Are you Mrs. Curtis?"

"Yes, I am," she said with a slight note of disdain.

"Is your husband Jack Curtis?"

"Yeah. Is he in trouble?"

"I'm afraid your husband's car was found overturned on the road into the village of Templeton. His car careered off the road and was found only a short time ago. The driver was killed. I'm afraid your husband is deceased. I'm very sorry."

May stood there and took everything in, or at least I think she did, it was hard to tell – her expression was totally blank.

"I'm going to need you to come to the mortuary in Mount Aerial Regional Hospital in order to identify the body," he said remorsefully.

"Of course," she replied, "Could you drive me, I'm a little over the limit," she lied.

"Certainly, but what about the girl?" he asked concerned.

"She'll be ok."

She flicked her head back to me.

"Go to bed, Ebony. Bring teddy with you." Then turning back to the guard she said, "I'll get the neighbour to keep an eye on her."

And with that they took off.

That was the beginning of my nightmare...

Matt O'Shea

SAMMIE THE ELF!

Tullamore Writing Group
14 years old
Chapter one of his novel
Sammie the Elf!

O nce upon a time there was a little elf called Sammie. He lived in a magical forest full of wonderful creatures, from magical elves to talking mushrooms! But there were also evil scary monsters in the dark part of the forest where the little elves never ventured.

Sammie was small and round like a tomato. He had little rosy cheeks, a big red nose and big pointy ears! He had a happy little life with all his elf friends in his happy little elf village! Or at least that's what he thought. The sad reality was that the villagers disliked Sammie. They were irritated by Sammie's overfriendliness and optimism. Sammie was also very clumsy. People felt nervous around him because he was always making mistakes. He often attracted mischief and trouble.

Sammie awoke one day, took a nice deep breath, savouring the forest air, sighed and said aloud to himself, "What a wonderful day! Not a cloud in the sky!"

He didn't mean this literally, because there were in fact clouds in the sky. He really meant that it was a nice day and there was nice weather. He then climbed out of his tree house and climbed to the top of the tree. He could hear the villagers below singing merrily to themselves. He glanced over the tops of the trees of the vast forest, the home of lots of little magical creatures!

Suddenly, a branch snapped under little Sammie's foot and he went tumbling down through the trees hitting several branches on the way down. Feet from the ground, his t-shirt snagged on a branch and he was left hanging from the tree!

"Ah, little help?" cried Sammie. "Get me down!"

"Well jeepers, Sammie!" came a dopey high pitched voice from behind Sammie. "Watcha doin' hangin' up in that there tree?"

The voice belonged to Sammie's best and only friend Chris. Chris was a dopey little elf who was equally despised by the other elves.

Sammie and Chris didn't fit in with the villagers because of their happy care-free simple lives, compared to the villagers' stuck up all-work-and-no-play attitude.

"I fell. Now just get me down," Sammie grunted.

"Well, ya didn't have ta snap," mumbled the offended Chris.

Chris climbed up the tree to where Sammie was hanging and snapped the branch, sending Sammie tumbling to the hard roots sticking up out of the ground below.

"Ouch," Sammie groaned, lying in a heap on the ground.

He got up rubbing his head.

Chris and Sammie decided to go to the centre of the village. Once there, Sammie and Chris headed for the candy shop!

"Two lolly pops, please," said Sammie merrily to the stern looking shopkeeper.

Sammie and Chris left the shop and stood in the busy street. Many people intentionally nudged into Sammie as they passed along the street, but he simply smiled and apologised politely. One Elf, who particularly disliked Sammie, knocked into him so hard he fell back into a fresh steaming pile of pony shit.

"Oh dear," mumbled Sammie. "Now I'm all stinky."

"Well golly, Sammie," said Chris, grabbing Sammie's hand to help him up, "You ought to go down to the river and wash off. You're awfully smelly!"

"Good idea," grinned Sammie.

And off they went to the river singing merrily as they skipped.

Once there, Sammie jumped in the river to clean all the shit off himself while Chris sat on the bank fishing. Sammie saw something glisten on the bed of the shallow river. He fished it out of the water.

"Hey, Chris, look what I found!"

It was a small rock, encrusted with what seemed to be a big emerald.

"Wow," said Chris, dumfounded by this strange gem, "that's probably worth a whole lot!"

"We should bring it back to the village and see how much it's worth,"

Sammie said, and they both started jumping up and down singing, "we're going to be rich" and skipped back to the village.

Sammie walked through the village carrying this strange stone with him. Suddenly, one of his elf 'friends' stuck out his foot and tripped Sammie up. Sammie fell to the ground sending the stone flying out of his hands. It flew high above the village and stayed there, suspended in mid air, gleaming under the sun. All the elves in the village looked up in the air at this fascinating sight, when suddenly, the stone let out a burst of light, shocking the crowds of elves below it, and burst into flames!

The fire fell upon the village and the now screaming crowds of elves rushed to the river with buckets to collect water to extinguish the fire, trampling over poor Sammie and Chris in the process.

It was chaos. The blaze spread like a forest fire... which is what it was...

Luckily, the fire was stopped before it did too much harm to the forest. "SAMMIE!" screamed Max, the mayor of the elves.

"This time we've had it! You and Chris are banned from this village, and are never to return."

"But..." Sammie started, tears filling his little puppy-dog eyes.

"Get out!" screamed Max. "And take your shit-smelling clothes with you."

So Sammie and Chris went to pack up their things, and off they went, walking along the banks of the river, singing and skipping and smelling of shite.

Aideen Hogg

PURPLE

*Kilbeggan Writing Group
16 years old
Short Story*

C harity rose from the wet cobbled ground beneath her, her knee dripping with blood. Her head felt light, too light, as though it was floating by itself. She reached up her grazed hand to investigate if it was still there, literally. A sudden urge ruptured in her stomach and she released, coughing up blood and a loose tooth. The vision of blood, her blood, sent Charity warning signs. It had all begun with just the name calling but this, this was too far.

She hobbled out of the alleyway. Her knee throbbed.

"Kick her harder."

Charity remembered the group of giggling girls, the cackling echoing through the empty alley. Their smirk grins and thrilled expressions had pierced into her mind. Charity felt as though all the thudding kicks had punctured her lungs.

"One more year," she sighed aloud.

Charity wasn't sure whether she could continue hiding this for another year. Could she really go through more attacks without saying a word?

As she walked through the street heading for home Charity caught her reflection in a window. The ghostly shaded girl staring back did not represent Charity, not the real Charity. Gone was the out-going bubbly girl and in her place was this quiet, timid shadow.

Old Charity had been replaced by a complete stranger.

She wiped the blood off her face as best she could but her cuts stung with the contact of her jumper. She knew she wouldn't be able to hide this from her mother.

The aroma of her mother's cooking immediately hit Charity when she walked through the front door. Her little brother Tony raced through the hallway with his arms spread wide. He wrapped them around his sister; Charity flinched in pain from her brother's tight grasp. He was so caught up in the excitement of his sister's return that he was oblivious at first to her bloodied clothes and the deep gash on her forehead.

"Eww," he squealed. "What's that?" he asked, pointing to the mark on her head.

At four years old Tony still had that baby tone in his voice.

"Tony, who are you talking to?"

Charity's mother poked her ginger head out the kitchen doorway.

"Charity!" she shrieked, seeing her bloodied daughter standing in the hallway. "What happened?"

Charity felt repulsed, not just because of her previous beating but because of her mother's fake worrying act, or so Charity thought.

"Nothing, mum, just leave it."

"Leave it! You're covered in blood! What happened? Who did this to you?"

"Just forget it."

Charity headed upstairs.

"Tell me, Charity," insisted her mother firmly.

"Why? Why do you decide to care now, mum? I'm surprised you even noticed, what with you being so busy."

"That's not fair. I do my best for you kids. But with your dad gone..."

The tears from Charity's eyes caused her cuts to sting but it was impossible to fight them.

"Of course, blame dad for all of this. For once, mum, I just want to be left alone. I don't need your help."

Charity walked into the crowded classroom. All eyes were on her, all eyes on the deep gash on her forehead. A snigger erupted somewhere at the back and Charity guessed who it was.

"Ouch," mocked Alex, the leader of the gang. "That looks sore, what happened?"

Charity brushed past her, aiming to take her seat but Alex stopped her in her tracks.

"I'm talking to you. I don't think you want another mark on your head, do you?"

Inside, Charity felt as though lava was churning, her cheeks turned red in anger.

Everyone took their seats and the teacher began, but throughout the English class, the class Charity once loved, she desperately tried to ignore the paper balls bashing against the back of her head and the rupture of whispered laughter afterwards.

"I'll be back in a moment," exclaimed the English teacher.

Charity's heart collapsed. She dreaded to think of what the girls would do next with Miss Stevens absent from the classroom. And it wasn't as though charity was going to cry out for help.

"There's funny little stories going around about you, or should I say about your father."

Charity shut her eyes tightly, hoping that somehow Alex would disappear. There was no need for Alex to fill her in on these little stories; Charity had heard them before. How her father had found a new girlfriend almost as young as Charity herself and how he had been having an affair behind Charity's mother's back for years of their marriage.

"Something about a teenage lover..." Alex continued.

The volcano inside Charity exploded.

"Shut up, just shut up," she screamed.

The classroom went dead silent.

"Well, Charity, I'm just saying what I heard and what I heard was..."

Charity viciously plunged towards Alex knocking them both onto the ground.

"What is going on?"

Miss Stevens rushed into the classroom, pulling the two girls apart.

Charity wriggled into the seat at the back of the bus. Every so often someone would turn around to look at Charity and whisper something to their partner. She dug inside her bag and cursed herself for forgetting her ipod. Music was her escape from all the drama in her life. The headphones deep inside her ears blaring the lyrics of a Tori Amos tune would take her away from everything, at least for a while.

The angry expression on Miss Stevens' face was drilled into her memory. Charity had never once had a teacher disappointed with her. Alex had put on her fake personality and persuaded Miss Stevens that both girls were simply messing. Miss Stevens had believed her.

There was another reason charity found it pointless confiding in people about her bullies. Alex had a way with words and, if she wanted, could probably convince people that *she* was the victim in all this.

As Charity stepped off the bus her mouth dropped. Four girls were standing in front of her.

"Well, look who it is. What a coincidence," smirked Alex. "Now, Charity, I'm still finding it difficult to forgive you for that vicious attack."

Alex wrapped her arm extra tightly around Charity's shoulder. Charity shook her grip off.

"Hey, if it wasn't for me you would be in so much trouble," grinned Alex.

"Oh is this where I thank you for being so generous. I would never have attacked you if you just stayed away from me."

Alex took hold of Charity's arm and the others followed. They dragged her into the porch of a run down house and pinned her up against the wall.

"This is for talking to me the way you just did."

The first punch felt the worst but the second sent a strange feeling through Charity's body. She felt it move up toward her neck and she choked out. Alex jumped back.

"Eww" Alex squealed. "Let's go. I don't want her vomiting on me."

That morning Charity woke from her warm bed. In the mirror she looked back at the girl with the bruises covering her body. She lifted up her pyjama top to examine the mark left behind by Alex. It was deep purple in colour; it looked a lot worse than it actually felt. Was she becoming immune to the beatings so much that she barely felt them?

The silver glint, something reflecting the sunlight, immediately caught Charity's attention. She looked down at the sink. There it was, right where she'd left it last night. She'd left it there to remind herself not to forget it. Charity took hold of its wooden handle; it felt snug in her hand. The sharp edge made her feel a sense of uncertainty but Charity ignored her feelings. She turned and slid the blade into her bag.

Charity felt today was going to be a different, better day. The knife made her feel protected. Something she hadn't felt in a long time. It wasn't as though she was going to use the knife, no; it was just a scare tactic.

In English, Charity felt Miss Stevens' glare baring down upon her, it made her feel uneasy. She kept her head down the entire class trying to ignore her teacher's scowl. Finally the bell went and the students poured out of the classroom.

"Charity" called Miss Stevens.

What now? It wasn't as though she done anything wrong. She'd kept her head down all through class.

"Yes, Miss Stevens."

Charity presented her most polite tone of voice.

"Is everything okay?"

Miss Stevens tucked her blonde lock behind her ear.

"What I mean is, is everything okay in school?"

Something triggered inside Charity. Now she had a chance to pour out the whole truth, let all the hurt inside her out.

Charity simply shrugged.

"Yes. Everything's fine."

"It's just that you seem a little..."

Charity cut her teacher off.

"Seriously, Miss Stevens, I'm fine. I better go."

She shot her English teacher a quick smile before she headed out the door. How much longer could she keep hiding this? How much longer could she pretend everything was okay?

As she walked up the street and turned into the alleyway, Charity's heart beat so fast in her chest that she could hear it. Well it was either that or the sudden pulse in her head. This was her chance to finally scare her tormentors away; soon she would be free of them. But what if the whole idea backfired? What if they simply laughed at her? What if somebody got hurt?

As Charity walked further down the alleyway, she started to doubt her plan. She started to hope that the girls wouldn't even be here, but her new hopes were crushed when she found them standing in a line, forming a barricade in front of her.

Charity pushed the knife further up her sleeve.

"Well, here was me thinking you were scared of us. But here you are, coming at us all on your own like a big girl. You're not very clever, are you, Charity?"

Charity's heart pounded in her chest. Her hands started to sweat.

What if the knife slipped out of her hand? What if Alex picked it up and used it?

Charity slipped the blade down into her palm.

She suddenly whipped it up in front of Alex.

"Alex, if you don't..."

Her hand began to shake uncontrollably.

"If you don't leave me..."

The knife would drop for sure; Charity was shaking and sweating so bad. She expected Alex to explode laughing but she just stood there – speechless, panic-stricken.

"Charity, what are you doing?"

"Shut up for once. I'm going to talk."

The coward inside Charity had disappeared. She was a little afraid of herself now. The knife gave her unlimited power.

"I'm sick of you telling me what to do. I'm sick of you hitting me when you feel like it and I'm sick of being scared of you."

"Charity, just think about what you're doing," pleaded Alex.

Alex's friends were frozen solid too.

"I know exactly what I'm doing."

Charity was finally standing up for herself.

"Please, Charity."

A tear slid away from the corner of Alex's eye.

"Not so nice feeling like this, is it? What's going to happen? Will you get hurt or not?"

Charity leapt forward. The girls behind Alex shrieked. She stopped right in front of Alex.

That was enough.

She had got what she wanted; she had scared her bullies.

So why was she still holding the knife?

Charity felt that if she dropped the knife it would show she had given up, returned to being the coward she always was. As long as she held the knife she was the one in control.

"Charity, we were just messing with you. It was all just a joke."

Charity lifted up her top.

"Is this just a joke?" she asked, revealing her bruised body.

Even Alex was shocked by the mess she'd created.

"I'm so sorry. I'll do anything," Alex insisted.

Now it was her turn. Now Alex was the vulnerable girl who begged her bullies to stop kicking her, biting her, hitting her. But one had ever listened to Charity's pleas. No. They only ever beat her up until she was this frozen, motionless mess.

So why should Charity listen to Alex?

Alex suddenly turned. She tripped, almost falling to the ground, and raced out of the alleyway. The other girls legged it in different directions. Charity sped after Alex. She was only interested in Alex.

She wanted Alex to feel the pain she had felt for months, wanted to give her a taste of her own medicine. Charity ran faster.

Thud!

The vision of Alex sprawled across the road immediately caused Charity to halt. Alex's body was limp on the road. Blood trickled from her ear forming a pool underneath her face.

A car door swung open. The driver got to his knees to check Alex's pulse. He shouted something out loud – his voice was panicked. Charity was instantly aware of how bad it was. A crowd of people rushed to Alex's side.

Charity felt as though she was back on the bus with the whispers and the stares. I was only supposed to be a simple scare tactic. Nobody was supposed to get hurt. She stood on the footpath still holding the knife by her side. She let in drop. The sound of the blade clanging off the ground ran through her ears.

She was now a human cast in stone, unable to speak, unable to move.

Aoife Gunning

SUMMER IS A LIE

Kilbeggan Writing Group
15 years old
Chapter one of her novel
Last Summer

Sarah tossed and turned, sweat rolling down her face.

"No! No!"

Her eyes were tightly closed.

"Sarah? Sarah? Are you up?"

Sarah jolted awake. She sat up panting like she'd run a mile. She rubbed her face with the sleeve of her top.

"Sarah you're going to be late," came from downstairs.

"Coming," she shouted back.

Sarah lazily got out of bed and strolled over to the white painted wardrobe, trying not to trip over the hundreds of shoes and clothes lying on the floor, like dead bodies scattered after a big battle. She put on the first thing she saw, a Nike sweater and a pair of dirty O'Neill's. Sarah wasn't fussed if clothes were clean or dirty.

"Sarah, your breakfast is cold and you're late!" her dad shouted.

"I'm here," she replied, walking into the brightly lit kitchen.

"You look upset. What's wrong?" her dad asked, putting a fry down on the table in front of her.

"Nothing really, it's just I had the dream again," Sarah muttered, just loud enough so it would penetrate over the noise of the fan.

"What dream is that?"

Her dad was moving about, getting ready for work.

"You know, the one where we're at the hospital waiting outside the theatre for the Doctor to tell us what's..."

Her dad abruptly interrupted her.

"Damn it! Come on, you'll miss the bus. You can tell me the rest when I come home from work".

Sarah went and got her bag.

Ring! Ring!

"Hello, Tom Reilly here."

Her father answered his mobile hurriedly.

Sarah slammed the door behind her and ran for the big yellow school bus. When she got o!, she went over to the two people standing near one of the oak trees beside the school entrance.

"Hey retards, any news?" Sarah asked as she reached them, giving each a hug.

"Jeez, I feel like I haven't seen ye in ages," said Ben.

"It's only been a few weeks," replied Amy. "So, Sarah, how's things?"

The three of them sat down outside on the steps watching everyone going inside.

"I had a dream last night," Sarah said.

"Oh my god, that reminds me, did ya hear about Alicia Rigney?" Amy gasped hysterically.

"No! I had that dream about being..."

Sarah tried to tell them about her dream but Amy obviously needed to get her story out first.

"Well, Alicia was at that camp she always goes to and it was night-time, right! Well, some of the girls put her hand in a basin of water and she wet herself."

Amy and Ben rolled around laughing.

Sarah squeezed out a smile.

"That's great! But I need to tell you about last night. I had the dream about..."

Dring. Dring.

The school bell eroded away what Sarah was going to say.

Bloody hell! Am I going to get to tell anyone about my dream? Sarah thought as she went into the classroom.

Miss Quinny strolled in wearing her usual dusty suit and orange specs, her untamed blond hair everywhere.

"Right, now class quiet down! Is everyone here?" she asked looking around, but before she could continue the door opened and Sarah felt a shiver down her spine and butterflies in her stomach.

Miss Quinny didn't look up.

"Late as usual, James! Take a seat."

She pointed to the chair in front of her. Sarah watched James sit down. James was perfect. He was almost 6ft tall with blond hair and deep blue eyes. Every girl liked him, every girl except Amy.

Why doesn't she like him? Sarah wondered. I can't understand it.

Every time Sarah saw James she could hardly breathe.

"Right, I want you to write a poem reflecting your summer holidays," Miss Quinny stated.

The whole class started giving out.

"QUIET! You have thirty minutes to do this so start now. I will also be grading your pieces."

At nine thirty Miss Quinny shouted, "Right. Pens down."

Everyone jumped and put their pens down with several claps.

Amy was up first.

"My summer holidays," Amy began.

Sarah suddenly started to get a headache. The pain began as a pinch in the side of her head and spread to the back of her skull, until her whole head felt sore. Sarah held the side of her face trying to concentrate on what each student at the top of the room was reading.

"Very good, Emer. Now how about you, Sarah."

Sarah got up o! the seat and stumbled. She felt weak, her legs crumbling beneath her.

God!

She swallowed hard and made herself walk forward. With each step she took her heart beat faster and harder. She could feel all eyes on her.

Oh my god, please say he isn't looking at me. Please don't be looking at me.

She glanced up, James was looking at her.

It seemed an eternity before Sarah finally reached the top of the classroom.

"Summer is a lie," she began. "Summer is a lie, we all make empty promises."

The words blurred on the page. Sarah blinked, swallowing back the pain drilling its way from one side of her skull to the other.

What the hell was wrong with her?

"We all make promises of meeting up but we never go through with them," she continued. "We never go through with them... we never..."

Sarah felt her whole body go numb. Her eyes were heavy. Instead of looking down at the class, her eyes were staring at the ceiling. She couldn't move. Everything faded away. Somehow she could still hear. Far away in the distance she heard the girls at the back of the room screaming hysterically and the boys laughing intently. She heard Miss

Quinny call her name. She heard Ben, Amy and James coming near her.

"Sarah! Sarah!" Miss Quinny called, gently rocking Sarah's lifeless body.

She felt Miss Quinny look for a pulse. No matter how hard she tried, Sarah couldn't speak. She couldn't move.

"She's alive," Miss Quinny gasped. "Her pulse is very weak. Amy, run to the office, get the principal..."

I'm alive, Sarah thought, trying to move her hands.

I'm trapped.

Michael Brady

IT'S NOT ME. IT'S YOU.

Tullamore Writing Group
17 years old
Excerpt from chapter one of his novel Insomnia

My sister Sophie was my favourite person in the world. She was the only female I had total respect for, she was an incredible person. My last memory of her was a conversation we had in the middle of the night. She warned me of the dangers of taking the people closest to me too seriously. Especially mother. I remember Sophie looking sad and full of thought as if her mind was at war with itself.

"Marcus," she said softly.

She had always called me Marcus since I was little. I could never remember why, it was just a thing we had. It separated us from everyone else.

"I want you to leave here as soon as you finish school. I know you're unhappy and you can't change that as long as you're still living here. Get out of California, find some real people, and most importantly forget everyone. Life isn't about jobs and money; it's about people and who you surround yourself with. What loves you does not define you; it's what you love that matters. Be free and be happy."

I remember asking, "Why are you telling me all of this?"

But I knew she was leaving. The next day she'd vanished. I persuaded my mother not to start an enquiry into her *beloved* missing daughter. The only reason the bitch wanted to go through the motions was so that people would think she actually cared. Think that she was the perfect, caring mother willing to do anything to find her daughter. Wrong. Mother hated Sophie like nothing else.

We never heard anything from Sophie again and I never got over it.

So twitchy. About this time of night is when I'm quite prone to mood swings or passing out. But I'm relatively in control. Flight to London departing in two hours. I left a note on the table for my mother to read. I got my point across. Mother won't try to find me. What's in it for her? I'm sure a part of her will be happy to see the end of me.

Might attempt some sleep on the plane, really not up to the effort though. For the past two years my insomnia has become increasingly worse. At first it scared me, but there's a lot I've come to love about insomnia. The average person spends a third of their life sleeping. I don't plan to live much longer than forty, but even still, what a waste. While the world sleeps, I stay awake, thinking. I get so much done. Every now and then I slide, fall into an uncomfortable sleep for maybe three hours but I never feel good after it. I'm on medication to help keep me stimulated and I must say it's good stuff. At the moment I'm so twitchy. It'll go away soon and I'll fall in to a beautiful ambient daydream where everything is soft and forgiving. What better place to experience this than at an airport?

Airports are magical. All those long white floors and the gentle hum of people's frantic bustle. Their panic, my sanctuary.

21 April 2004 San Francisco Airport, 1.05a.m.

I leaned against a pillar and let myself forget. Even though I was standing, something inside me sank into the airport floor. I came out the other side floating, no pain, no noise, no agonising conflict stabbing the inside of my head. Just quiet. All the twitching and uneasiness faded away, replaced by utter peace of mind and an inexplicable unawareness of my surroundings. A perfect trance. The marble floor and white pillars melted around me and in the distance on the edge of the white abyss were several lights, all where I wanted them to be. From this beautiful horizon an angel materialized, at least she seemed like an angel. She walked towards me, her arms fading in and out of focus, blurry against the cloudy background. Slowly she raised her hand. I looked up to see a girl standing over me, a nervous smile playing around her lips.

"Excuse me, did you drop this?"

She was holding a passport which was quite obviously mine. It bore my photograph for one thing. She had no idea how important her significance was right then. She was holding my ticket to possible freedom. The only explanation was that she was an angel. How could I repay her?

"I'm going to buy you coffee," I stated.

A true declaration of how forward and blunt a man can be. Well done sir, the greatest pick up line you'll ever come out with.

You idiot.

In retrospect, however, it seemed the most intelligent thing I would ever say to a girl.

"Oh, yes please, that would be really nice," she replied.

I gestured to the café behind the pillar and we both took our seats facing each other. She sat with her arms resting on the table and her legs on the ground. What woman who doesn't know a man decides *not* to cross her legs? I knew then she was unusual. It turned out she had been walking behind me for a long time and noticed me drop the passport. Instead of giving it to me immediately she decided to study it, to examine my face to see what I looked like from the front, eventually deciding to approach me with it.

I learned that her name was Sophie. This brought a tear to my eye, forcing me to think about my sister, whom I hadn't seen or spoken to in two years. Mother was and still is convinced she was kidnapped or killed, but I know Sophie is still alive.

This mysterious, angelic other Sophie told me her life story right there and then with astonishing openness and lack of fear.

"Do you know why I'm sharing all of this with you? You listen and you've no preconceptions."

Normally I hate people making judgements about me before they know me, but this was different, oh, it was so different. I was open to anything out of the ordinary and mundane in life and Sophie was out of the ordinary. Finally came the million-dollar question.

"What's your name?"

She did ask with sweet sincerity, so I replied.

"It's Yann, but you can call me Marcus."

"Why Marcus?" she responded.

"It's what my sister used to call me."

21 April 2004, Flight JY7345, 2.05 a.m.

An hour later found me sitting with a rare smile on my face. Window seat. Beautiful girl, too wonderful to be real, sitting beside me pouring her life story like warm water into my hands. Is anything better than a window seat at night? Makes you feel enlightened.

"That's the first time I've seen you smile," Sophie remarked.

"Of course I'm going to smile, right now I've everything. Nothing up here is real. I'm in a dream world."

She replied quickly.

"You don't mean that literally, do you? You feel that when we land and you step o! the plane, that's reality?"

All the time you dream of meeting someone who knows what to say at exactly the right moment, someone who actually gets you. But when it happens it seems too good to be true.

"Yes," I said, taken aback. "That's exactly what I mean. Maybe I think you'll just disappear when the plane lands, and then I'll have to go back to feeling like a fifteen year old girl."

She laughed and shook her head.

"Despite your odd comparison to yourself and teenage girls, which by right should scare away most people, I promise not to disappear. If you want you can stay with me for a while before you meet your friend and we could get to know each other?"

Usually it was me that asked females questions like that.

"Get to know you?" I questioned jokingly. "I feel like I've known you all my life. If marriage wasn't so frightening and I didn't know any better I'd propose right now."

She laughed.

She was a breath of fresh air. How long does fresh air last though?

"Where are you staying?" I asked.

"Just with some friends, they've a nice place right in the centre of the city."

"Will they mind?" I asked. "I don't want to be intrusive or anything."

"You'll realise how funny that question is when you meet my friends," Sophie grinned. "They're, well, they're carefree and wild, always anxious to meet new people."

The thought of meeting a large group of new people, who had no idea who I was, seemed the most exciting thing I could do with my life right now, aside from sitting beside this little angel playing catch with the good vibes. The plane had to land sometime, so I agreed. I wasn't going to turn down the possibility of spending the night lying beside Sophie.

"Sophie?" I whispered softly.

She rested her head on my shoulder.

"Yes, Marcus?"

"Something amazing is about to happen."

I think I said it more to myself but that's all I remember and for the first time I fell into an unforced, beautiful sleep. All because of her.

I woke up with Sophie shaking my arm and whispering to me.

"You look dead when you sleep. Dead, but happy. How do you feel?" she asked.

"Alive," I responded. "Very much alive."

I wasn't lying either. I felt amazing. The plane had stopped and people were standing up taking their baggage down from the racks above the seats, all like ants scurrying about their business. All in such a rush. That's Heathrow, one big rush full of scurrying ants.

Magical.

Michelle Murray

TWICE UPON A TIME

Kilbeggan Writing Group
16 years old
Short Story

For seven men, she gave her life,
For one good man, she was his wife,
Beneath the ice of Snow White falls,
There lies the fairest of them all.

Anna didn't have to go to work in the crèche this Saturday. Instead she went to the park where she met her best friends Ciara and Ryan.

"So she blamed you?!" Ciara exclaimed.

"Yeah," said Anna.

"But it wasn't your fault?"

"I dunno, thinking back maybe it was."

"Rubbish," Ryan exploded. "You don't move when someone's using a curling thongs on your hair, of course you're gonna get burned."

Ryan noticed the girls staring at him, a little worried that he knew so much about curling thongs.

"Or so I'd imagine," he said sheepishly.

They all burst out laughing.

He always knows how to cheer me up, thought Anna.

"Here, I'm starving,'" Ryan said in a rather manly voice. "Do ye want to get something to eat?"

The girls agreed and they were off.

A few laughs and a five minute walk later they were sitting at a table in a café.

"So, how come you got the day off work, part-time crèche girl?" Ryan asked, his mouth full of tuna sandwich.

"Nicole forgot to tell me she was taking my shift. I don't know if I'll go into child care after I finish school..."

Anna was suddenly distracted. Jake had just walked in. She completely zoned out of the conversation with her friends and totally focused on him.

Anna remembered the dream she had last night.

It was dark. She was in the park. The trees were beautifully lit by solar lights. Jake was there. She couldn't see his face but she knew it was him. He took her hand and they danced around their picnic and...

"Hello! Earth to Anna!" Ryan said, slightly nudging her.

"It's no use," Ciara shook her head, "She's thinkin' about Jake."

"Jake?" Anna said, zoning back in. "What?"

"See!" Ciara said, slightly amused by her friend.

"I don't know what you see in him," Ryan complained, shrugging his shoulders.

Oh god! He's gorgeous. Ryan doesn't get it. Ok, Anna, be cool, pretend to Jake that you don't even notice him. Yes, that's it. Damn, oh god, did he see me looking at him! Ok, act natural.

Anna took a bite of her sandwich.

"Hiyas," Jake said, walking over.

Anna looked up and stared into Jake's clear green eyes.

Oh shit, thought Anna, panicking. She had egg hanging out of her mouth from the huge bite she'd taken from her sandwich. Oh god, oh god, oh god, think fast Anna.

She picked up a napkin and spit out the mouthful of egg.

"Oh hey, Jake," Anna smiled, desperately hoping she wasn't going red. "What's up?"

"Nothing much. Y'know the usual," Jake grinned. "I was just on my way home. Actually I'm late," he said, looking at his watch. "I'll see yis at school".

"Ok, bye," Ciara waved.

"God he's gorgeous," Anna whispered, biting her lower lip.

Ryan rolled his eyes.

"So, have you decided what you want for your birthday?" he asked, desperate to change the subject.

"Not yet," Anna said, dreamily taking a sip of her drink.

Anna was sitting on the bridge in the park across from her house. She couldn't bring herself to go in.

God, just go in. What's the worst that could happen? Ok, she'll shout at you and give you the guilt trip, but then it will be over!

Anna was still battling with herself when she reached her front door. Fishing for her keys, the door suddenly opened and there she was, Anna's stepmother Scarlett. Scarlett was barely noticeable in the doorway she was so thin. She had tied up her dyed blonde hair to make the burn on her neck very noticeable.

Stupid cow, thought Anna.

Anna knew what her step-monster was like. Scarlett was a serpent that slithered around looking for attention and trouble.

"Come in out of the cold, Anna," Scarlett said in her nicest voice.

Anna stepped in the doorway to find her dad standing in the hall. Her stepmother gave a sly smile.

"Scarlett told me what happened this morning," her dad said calmly.

He wasn't really the type to give out, even though he was a lawyer and made a living from admonishing people.

"I'm sorry, dad," Anna said, matching her father's calm tone, "but it wasn't really my fault."

"This wasn't your fault!" Scarlett chimed in, showing the mark were the curling thongs had burnt her. "How is this not your fault?" she shouted. "I'm going to be scarred for life."

Scarlett was exaggerating, her botoxed face twisting into what might have been an expression of anger.

"Calm down, Scarlett," Anna's dad said. "Let's see what Anna has to say about it. Anna?"

He looked down at Anna, she looked up at him. Her father was a good seven inches taller than her.

"Scarlett asked me to curl her hair. When I was doing it she turned her head," Anna said simply.

By now Scarlett was clenching her fists. She knew her husband was taking Anna's side.

"Ok, I think this has all been a misunderstanding."

Anna's father turned to look at his raging wife.

"Scarlett, it wasn't done on purpose."

"She burned my flesh," Scarlett cried.

It will go nicely with the two slits behind your ears, where your face has been stapled back, thought Anna.

"I'm sorry, Scarlett," Anna apologised, and left it at that. "Can I go to my room?" she asked.

"Yeah, go on," her dad said.

God, they've only been married for three months. I don't know how much more of this I can take, thought Anna, as she sauntered up the stairs.

"Anna," her dad called her back.

"Yeah?" she asked, turning on the stairs.

"You look very pretty today," he said.

This was something he told Anna often. She figured it was because she was so like her late mother. She could tell her dad still missed her mother and she also knew that he didn't feel the same way about Scarlett. Sure he liked Scarlett on some level but he only married her because he was so lonely. When Scarlett had moved in she'd taken all the pictures of Anna's mother down and replaced them with ones of herself.

"Thanks, dad," said Anna, and continued on up the stairs.

The next day went by really quite quick. Scarlett had gone about the day as if nothing had happened. The thing about Scarlett was she fought hard but she knew when a battle was lost. She kept looking at the burn on her neck in the mirror, but Scarlett always looked in the mirror at herself, so Anna didn't take much notice. Things were tense at dinner, with her dad the only one trying to make conversation.

That night, Scarlett came into Anna's room.

"I thought I'd give you an early birthday present to smooth things over and lighten the mood a little," Scarlett smiled her sugary smile.

She handed Anna a neatly wrapped gift.

Oh god, what's this? It's gotta be alcohol. She's gonna tell my dad I've been drinking. No, it'll be a box of rats or spiders. I wouldn't put anything past her.

"Go on, open it," Scarlett pointed to the box.

Anna could feel the sweat trickling along her palms. She unwrapped the gift as slowly as possible, trying to put off whatever fate her step-monster had in store for her.

Finally she lifted the lid off the cardboard box, inside was a magnificent golden comb filled with jewels and a pastel blue corset.

"Oh Scarlett!" Anna exclaimed, feeling a pang of guilt in the pit of her stomach. "They're beautiful, thank you."

"I thought you'd like them. Here, let me help you put them on."

"Ok," Anna agreed, surprised that her stepmother was making an effort.

Anna put the corset on and Scarlett helped her lace it up. Scarlett pulled the laces harder and harder until Anna grew short of breath. The corset squeezed her tight. Her ribs were being crushed, and her crushed bones were sticking into her delicate organs.

"S... S... Scarlet, I... I think that's tight enough."

Scarlett continued to pull, tighter and tighter. She only stopped when Anna collapsed onto the floor. Scarlett ran out of the room screaming. Anna furiously tugged at the strings of the corset but they only became tighter. Suddenly Anna's dad came running into her room. He untied the laces. Anna gasped for air.

"Are you all right?" her Dad asked, helping her to sit up.

Oh my god! I can't believe he's even asking that, he saw the state I was in, thought Anna.

"Yeah, dad, I'm fine," she lied.

"What happened?" he asked.

"The laces were tied too tight," Anna answered, not wanting to say what really happened because she wasn't even sure what'd really happened.

"Ok," said her dad, not wanting to press.

"This is nice," he said, taking up the comb that Scarlett had given Anna.

He put it in Anna's ebony black hair.

"You look lovely."

He brushed back a strand of hair from her face.

"It's late, Anna," he said. "You should go to bed."

As Anna was getting ready for bed she felt unwell.

Oh god, she thought, as the pain seeped through her body and her breaths became short. What's happening to me? Oh god. Oh god. Anna collapsed onto the floor for the second time that Sunday. As she fell, the comb dislodged from her hair and tumbled onto her bed. Lying on the floor, watching a tiny spider climb across her fingers, Anna slowly began to feel better.

The pain is gone, she thought, getting up. As Anna regained her balance she noticed the comb on the bed. She picked it up and put it into a drawer.

The next morning Anna woke up, got dressed, had breakfast and went to school, the same as always. When she was sitting in class, gossiping with Ryan and Ciara before the teacher started lessons, a woman came into the classroom.

"Could I see Anna Neige please?" said the woman.

"Certainly," Mr Hayes nodded.

Anna got up and left the classroom with the woman.

"Don't worry, you're not in any trouble," the woman reassured Anna. "This is my room."

They came to a door that read *Wilhelmina Grimm – School Counsellor*. The woman opened the door and gestured to Anna to go in. Sitting at her desk, Wilhelmina began to ask questions.

"How are you getting on in school, Anna?"

"Fine," Anna said.

"Has anything peculiar happened to you recently?" Wilhelmina asked calmly examining Anna's face.

Oh god! What does she know? Its ok, Anna, act cool, you can do this. "No."

Anna tried to keep the panic out of her eyes.

"Ok, Anna, I'm going to be perfectly honest with you. I think it's time I introduced myself. I am Wilhelmina Grimm, descendant of the one and only Grimm Brothers."

"Oh, good for you! But what does that have to do with me?" Anna asked.

"Everything!" said Wilhelmina. "What do you know about the Grimm fairytale of Snow White?" she asked, still examining Anna's face intently.

"Eh... had evil stepmother, lived with dwarves, ate poisoned apple, died, got kissed by a prince and they all lived happily ever after like every other Grimm fairytale," Anna said confused.

"Well..." Wilhelmina paused, and then tapping her fingers together she continued, "It's a true story. Snow White. My ancestors were there and wrote the whole thing down. Grimms never lie."

"So it's a true story..." Anna prompted.

"Which means in every generation a new Snow White is born. This time it's you."

Wilhelmina waited for Anna's reaction.

"Yeah, ok, is it time to take your pills?" Anna frowned.

Wilhelmina was obviously mad.

"I thought you might be like this," Wilhelmina smiled sadly.

Ok, Anna thought, how am I gonna get out of here? I can't just run for it, but then again, I might have to.

"Anna, I'm not crazy."

"Can I go now?" asked Anna, getting desperate.

"Don't you understand? You're her, you're Snow White, well... the reincarnation."

"Listen lady, you've got the wrong person..." Anna began.

"No," Wilhelmina interrupted. "I have the right person. I've been studying you for a while. I mean, all you have to do is look at your name. Anna Blanche Neige! Blanche Neige means Snow White.

Anna frowned, what if Wilhelmina was right? She glared at the crystal unicorn on the table. What if she was Snow White?

"The corset," she whispered, "and the comb."

Wilhelmina nodded quietly, "Tell me."

Anna told her everything.

"I see, it has started."

Wilhelmina tapped the side of her head thoughtfully.

"In every generation the story plays out all by itself. I will be your adviser through this, but, if Snow White doesn't have a prince to kiss her, she will remain dead."

Prince? Anna's eyes widened. Of course, Jake. Jake is my prince. He's gonna kiss me, oh god I'd better start practicing. Oh god, Oh god, his soft lips. His soft hair, his... Hang on.

"Dead!?" Anna cried.

"Of course, that's if you do die. It'd be better to stop that from happening, don't you think, so let's see."

Wilhelmina counted on her fingers.

"You've had the corset, the comb. That's two down, one to go."

"What do you mean?" asked Anna.

"Now all that's left is the apple".

"Well I'm allergic to apples and I check everything I eat," said Anna.

"Ok. That makes it easier," said Wilhelmina, "But we will have to be vigilant."

At lunch time Anna found Ryan and Ciara at their usual spot by the stairs. She went over to them.

"Well, are you crazy then?" asked Ryan.

"No," Anna replied, she had already thought of her cover. "It's just one of those things to see how you're getting on in school. You'll probably get called in the next few days".

After school Anna went home and looked for everything they had on Snow White. She found a book which she read intently, and a Disney video which she watched over and over again.

That night Anna got a call.

"Hey Anna, it's me. Do you know what maths homework we have?"

Anna felt her stomach do a summersault. It was Jake.

He called me for the maths homework. He could have called anyone. He called me! This has to be a sign. He's my prince. Ok, act cool.

"Oh hey yeah, it was number two on page 356," she said.

"Thanks Anna, you're the best," Jake replied and hung up.

Anna was still recovering from the call when she phoned Ciara and Ryan on her three way calling system. Anna told them about Jake, going on and on about it until finally Ryan had had enough and hung up.

"What's with him?" Anna asked Ciara.

"I dunno, he's a fella," she said but Ciara knew exactly what was wrong with Ryan.

Over the next few days Wilhelmina taught Anna all about Snow White and ways to avoid the dreaded apple.

"Now Anna, there's something I need to tell you," Wilhelmina said during their meeting on Saturday morning before Anna went to work.

"No Snow White since the original one was ever woken from the dead. All the other Snow White's are still, you know, slumbering in a coffin."

"Don't worry, I have my prince," Anna chirruped.

"You sound pretty sure," said Wilhelmina. "This prince of yours, does he love you as much as you love him?"

"Eh...."Anna began to get worried.

Jake had never actually said that he liked her. But it's not like he hasn't dropped hints, thought Anna.

"I don't know," she shrugged, "but I will find out... I'll find out tonight," she said determinedly.

Anna made her way towards the door.

"Oh Anna," Wilhelmina called her back.

"Yeah?" said Anna turning around.

"Happy Birthday."

"Oh...thanks," Anna smiled.

With all the hard work she was doing she had completely forgotten about her birthday. Anna had an hour before she went to work, she decided to call Jake and get it over with.

Anna sat at the cafe table waiting for Jake. She was nervous about what would happen. Did Jake feel the same way about her as she did about him?

Jake arrived and sat down.

"Heya," Anna said.

"Heya," Jake grinned.

It was clear he didn't know what was going on.

Ok, Anna, just go for it. Worst case scenario, he doesn't feel the same way.

"Jake," Anna began "I'm just going to say it. I like you."

"Yeah, I like you too," he replied.

"No, Jake... I *really* like you," Anna blurted out, waiting breathlessly for Jake's response.

Yes, Anna I love you too, that's all you have to say, come on Jake. You can do it.

"Oh... eh," Jake began, when a tall red-haired girl came up to the table.

"Hey, babe, are you nearly ready?" she asked, looking at Anna.

"Oh yeah," Jake said, as he kissed the girl on the cheek.

"Anna... this is my girlfriend, Orlaith... Hun, this is my friend Anna," Jake said, getting up.

"Hi," said Orlaith.

"Hi" said Anna.

She could feel her eyes welling up.

Just tell them you have a date. Yeah that will make him jealous. No, stupid, you have to go to work, just say you have to go to work.

"I have to go to work," announced Anna. "It was nice to meet you."

She smiled at Orlaith as she got up and left as quickly as she could.

"Anna," Jake called after her but she was too embarrassed to turn around.

Anna didn't let herself cry until she was out of Jake's sight, then she let it all out.

How could I be so stupid? Of course a guy like him is bound to have a girlfriend. Why didn't I even think about that?

Anna wiped her eyes before she went to work in the crèche. She didn't want the kids to see her crying again. When she finally got to the crèche, it was empty.

She found a note from Jade.

Anna, took the kids to the park. Be back soon. Jade x.

The phone rang, it was Wilhelmina.

"Heya," said Anna.

"Are you all right, Anna? You sound like you've been crying," said Wilhelmina.

"Yeah, I'm fine. I don't have a prince, but I'm fine."

"Oh dear, I'm sorry. He didn't feel the same way?"

"No."

Anna could feel the tears coming again.

"What are you going to do?" asked Wilhelmina.

"I have no idea."

"Don't worry, we'll think of something."

But Anna knew from her tone that Wilhelmina was as scared.

"Why don't I come over? See if we can't hatch a plan?"

"I'm at the crèche."

"Ok, see you in a bit."

Anna was cleaning up the crèche waiting for Wilhelmina to arrive when her stepmother walked in.

"Hello, Anna," said Scarlett in her usual high pitched tone.

Anna whirled around.

"You look surprised to see me," said Scarlett taking a bag from behind her back.

"What do you want?" asked Anna, trying so hard to sound polite.

After all, her stepmother knew nothing about the whole Snow White thing.

"Well, you left so early this morning that I couldn't give you your birthday present."

"But you already gave me my present," said Anna, remembering the corset and the comb.

"That was only a token gift," smiled Scarlett. "This is your *real* present."

"Ok," said Anna, "leave it on the table."

"God, Anna, I am trying to make an effort here. The least you could do is open it in front of me."

Anna knew she was probably coming across as rude but she had to be careful. There could be an apple in that bag. Anna turned around hoping her stepmother would go away. Instead, Scarlett took the present out of the bag and sprayed it on Anna.

A fine mist of perfume settled on Anna's pale skin. She felt weak.

Oh god, I'm dizzy.

Anna turned, squinting at the bottle in her stepmother's hand. She saw the label.

DKNY Apple Perfume.

Too late, Anna thought, sinking to the floor, her ebony black hair falling over her shoulder, her porcelain skin draining to snow white and her red lips turning blue. Anna felt a knot in her throat, she couldn't breath, she was choking, her eyes closed.

Snow White was dead.

Ten minutes later Ryan was at the door of the crèche, he knew he had to apologise for hanging up the phone with no reason last night. After a long discussion with Ciara, he'd decided to finally tell Anna how he felt about her.

Ryan was at the door practicing what he was going to say when Wilhelmina approached.

"Hello. Are you a friend of Anna's?" she asked.

"Yeah," said Ryan. "Hey, you're that counsellor. The one from school. What are you doing here?" he asked.

"I'm just seeing how Anna is. Why are you here?"

"Oh," Ryan sighed, "I have to apologise, see I kinda hung up on her last night. She needs an explanation."

"Oh right," Wilhelmina paused. "Have you and Anna been friends for a while?"

"Yeah. A long time. She's all obsessed with this guy Jake!" Ryan said.

"And that annoys you?"

"Well... .you see..."

"Oh my god, you're in love with her," exclaimed Wilhelmina.

"How come everyone else can tell except Anna?" asked Ryan.

"Well, are you going to go in and tell her?" asked Wilhelmina, nodding towards the door.

Ryan opened the door to find Anna motionless on the floor. Scarlett was mute, standing shaking, staring at the bottle in her hand.

"Oh my god," Ryan ran to Anna and knelt down beside her.

"What do we do?" he asked Wilhelmina.

"Kiss her."

"I don't know CPR. I've never done mouth to mouth. I can't do the counting thing."

"No," Wilhelmina patted his shoulder, "I mean *kiss* her."

Ryan looked at Wilhelmina as if she was crazy.

"If you don't kiss her she will remain dead," Wilhelmina assured him. "Is that what you want?"

Ryan placed his lips on Anna's mouth and softly kissed her.

Within seconds Anna woke up to find her stepmother weeping, Wilhelmina standing at the door, and Ryan at her side.

She knew she had been saved. Ryan had kissed her. Ryan!

Anna sat up, grabbed Ryan's face and kissed him back.

"Thank you," she smiled shyly.

"Ok, what just happened?" asked Ryan.

Wilhelmina told Ryan everything about Anna, how she was really Snow White. He was shocked but seemed to believe her. He said he had to kiss Anna again and again to make sure. And he did make sure, kissing Anna again and again until she laughed gleefully.

"Well," Wilhelmina said, "It looks like you've found your prince."

Anna smiled and with Ryan's help she went home.

That night Anna went to the park. Ryan said he had a surprise for her. She found him on a blanket full of food, when he saw her coming, he stood up.

"Happy Birthday," he said.

Anna smiled.

Ryan turned on his CD player, took Ann's hand and they began to dance. He kissed Anna gently.

"So do you want your present?" he asked

"Of course," Anna beamed.

He took a velvet box out of his jacket pocket and gave it to Anna. She opened it. Inside glittered an apple necklace.

"Here's an apple you can actually have," Ryan said.

"Thank you," Anna exclaimed, flinging her arms around his neck.

"I love it," she said. "I love you."

Ryan was overcome with joy.

"I love you too," he said.

And they all lived happily ever after!

A Murder of Crows
is set in Celeste with
Univers 67 display.